Pitchers' Duel

The Chip Hilton Sports Series

For more information on
Chip Hilton-related activities and to correspond
with other Chip fans, check the Internet at
chiphilton.com

Chip Hilton Sports Series

#7

Pitchers' Duel

Coach Clair Bee

Updated by Randall and Cynthia Bee Farley
Foreword by Dean Smith

BROADMAN
& HOLMAN
PUBLISHERS

Nashville, Tennessee

0-8054-1989-6

Published by Broadman & Holman Publishers,
Nashville, Tennessee
Page Design: Anderson Thomas Design, Nashville, Tennessee
Typesetting: PerfecType, Nashville, Tennessee

Subject Heading: BASEBALL—FICTION / YOUTH
Library of Congress Card Catalog Number: 98-50758

Library of Congress Cataloging-in-Publication Data
Bee, Clair.
Pitchers' duel / by Clair Bee ; edited by Cynthia Bee Farley,
Randall K. Farley.
p. cm. — (Chip Hilton sports series ; v. 7)
Updated ed. of a work published in 1950.
Summary: During his senior year at Valley Falls High
School, Chip pitches in the state championship baseball
tournament, runs for student mayor, and fights a drive to
force Coach Rockwell to retire.
ISBN 0-8054-1989-6 (pbk.)
[1. Baseball—Fiction. 2. Coaches (Athletics)—Fiction.
3. High schools—Fiction. 4. Schools—Fiction.] I. Farley,
Cynthia Bee, 1952– . II. Farley, Randall K., 1952– .
III. Title. IV. Series: Bee, Clair. Chip Hilton sports
series ; v. 7.

PZ7.B381955Pi   1999
[Fic]—dc21   98-50758
                                                        CIP
                                                        AC

2 3 4 5 03 02 01 00

TO

GEORGE BOCK, M.D.

Whose love for baseball is exceeded
only by his loyalty to his profession

COACH CLAIR BEE
1950

TO

JOHN HUMPHREY

Thank you for your vision, your friendship, and your faith.
Your dedication to Clair Bee and Chip Hilton
kept the dream alive for others.

RANDY, CINDY, AND MIKE
1999

Contents

CONTENTS

Foreword

WHEN I WAS ten or eleven years old, as World War II started, I was forced to read books by my parents. Since I liked athletes, I read and enjoyed several books by John Tunis that dealt primarily with baseball, as well as sportsmanship. Now fast forward to the summer of 1959, when at long last I had the opportunity to meet acclaimed basketball coach Clair Bee.

Frank McGuire was a close friend of Coach Bee, and I had just finished my first year as an assistant to Coach McGuire at North Carolina. Coach Bee was helping Frank with his basketball books, *Offensive Basketball* and *Defensive Basketball*. They had asked me to select two topics for chapters in *Defensive Basketball,* so we spent a great deal of time together that summer at the New York Military Academy.

During this period, not only did I stare at the painting of the fictional folk hero—Chip Hilton—that was on the wall behind Coach Bee's dining room table, but I had the opportunity to read some of the Chip Hilton series. The books were extremely interesting and well written, using sports as a vehicle to build character. No one did that better than Clair Bee (although John R. Tunis came close). By that time, Bee's Chip Hilton books had become a classic series for youngsters. While Coach Bee was well known as one of the greatest coaches of all time, due to his strategy and competitiveness, I believe he thought he could help society and young people most by writing this series. In his eyes, it was his "calling" in the years following his college and professional coaching career.

Coach McGuire and I, along with countless other basketball coaches, learned basketball from Clair Bee. The point zone, which Coach Bob Spear and I developed at the Air Force Academy, had its origins in one of Coach Bee's old books on the 1-3-1 rotating zone defense. We made our point zone at Air Force to be more of a match-up zone, but this is just one instance where people on the basketball court today still depend on innovations by Clair Bee.

From 1959 until his death, I visited with Coach Bee frequently at the New York Military Academy and at Kutsher's Sports Academy, which he directed. He certainly touched my life as a special friend. Not only does he still rank at the top of his profession as a basketball coach, but he now regains the peak as a writer of sports fiction. I am delighted the Chip Hilton sports series has been redone to make it more appropriate for athletics today, without losing the deeper meaning of defining character. I encourage everyone to give these books as gifts to other young athletes so that Coach Bee's brilliant method of making sports come to life and of building character will continue.

DEAN E. SMITH

Head Coach (Retired), Men's Basketball,
University of North Carolina at Chapel Hill

CHAPTER 1

Bleacher Bums

THE LOWER and upper frames of the scoreboard on the right-field fence showed two long rows of goose eggs. It was the last of the sixth, one down, and the home team pitcher was at bat. The tall teenager standing just outside the first-base batter's box eyed the scoreboard a second, noted the count of two and one, and then pulled his bat through in a full left-handed swing. Anyone who knew baseball would have caught the significance of the level bat, the smooth, flowing swing, and the last-second snap of the wrists that denotes a natural hitter.

The blond athlete with the unsmiling gray eyes pulled his batting helmet a little lower over his right eye and stepped into the batter's box. Oblivious to the crescendo of cheers from the stands and the home team dugout, he poised the bat over his left shoulder and eyed the pitcher. The visiting hurler knew Chip Hilton and knew he was a hard long-ball hitter. He wasn't about to give his broad-shouldered pitching opponent anything good. He studied Hilton's wide stance and then caught the challenge in the hitter's steady gaze. That did it! He'd strike this guy out if he never pitched another game as long as he lived.

The ball came in, low and inside, and Chip let it go for a count of three and one. Stepping away from the plate, Chip's glance flickered to the third-base coaching box where Soapy Smith, cupped hands to his mouth, was jabbering away about certain "pitchers who can't find the plate."

Chip also noticed that Soapy's right foot was kicking dirt, the sign to take the next pitch. Chip sighed resignedly and stepped back into the box. He liked this advantage against the pitcher, but he knew "Rock" was right; it was late in the game, and Henry "Rock" Rockwell, Valley Falls's veteran coach, was playing for one run. He wanted Chip Hilton on base, and when you were playing for Coach Rockwell, you obeyed signs—or else!

Rick Parcels, Salem High School's star right-hander, wasn't going to walk Hilton if he could help it. He carefully placed a called strike right around Chip's knees for the full count. Again Chip stepped out of the box and flashed a look toward the third-base coaching box for the sign, but Soapy Smith seemed to have taken a sudden interest in Salem's left fielder. Soapy's back was toward the plate, and he was hollering and making faces at his new target. Chip knew he was on his own.

Parcels took a slow, full windup and then put everything he had on the three-and-two pitch. The fastball burned toward the plate waist-high. Chip's swing was perfectly timed, and he solidly spanked the ball on the bat's sweet spot. Chip had tagged that one! He'd met it right on the nose, pulling a slashing line drive toward right center. His follow-through pulled him around with the hit, and he dug his spikes in ever-lengthening strides as he tore along the path toward first base. Chet Stewart, Rockwell's assistant, was standing in the first-base coaching box waving him on. As Chip made the turn, he saw the Salem center fielder stab frantically at the bounding ball.

The right fielder, coming over to back up the play, suddenly reversed his direction to chase the deflected ball. That was enough for the speeding base runner. The Valley Falls High School state champions needed the run he carried, and they would have a good chance to get it if Chip Hilton could reach third. Chip really poured it on then. He tagged second without breaking stride and headed for the Salem third baseman, who was straddling the bag with hands outstretched toward the throw from right field. Chip knew it was going to be close.

Soapy Smith was down on his knees in the third-base coaching box, arms extended toward the bag with palms down, screaming, "Hit the dirt, Chip! Hit the dirt!"

Twelve feet from the bag, Chip took off in a headlong dive, arms reaching desperately for the bag. His hands met the base a split second before the gloved ball dug viciously into his back. Chip got to one knee, holding his breath, afraid to look at the base umpire. An explosive roar from the home stands greeted the decision, and Chip knew he was safe. He scrambled to his feet, brushing the dirt from his uniform, happy he'd set up the run that the Big Reds needed so badly. He flashed a quick smile at Soapy and glanced toward the dugout. Coach Rockwell caught the glance and thundered in Chip's direction.

"Atta boy, Chipper! Atta boy!"

Everyone in the park knew the play now. The Big Reds' coach would squeeze this run in now, for sure! In spite of Parcels and his clever pitching, that's exactly what Rockwell did. In the conference on the mound, the Salem coach talked earnestly to Parcels. The Salem infield was moved in with the obvious intention of cutting off the run at the plate.

Parcels pitched them high and low to Cody Collins, with Chip breaking toward the plate with every throw and back to third when the ball thudded into the catcher's glove. Then, on the three-and-no count, Collins met a low pitch and dumped a perfect bunt down the third baseline. Chip, sliding headlong under and past the catcher who was trying to block the plate, was in for the first run of the game almost as soon as Parcels had fielded the ball. The Salem pitcher didn't even try for the play at the plate, and his hard throw barely nipped a speeding Cody at first for the second out. After Speed Morris, the Big Reds' flashy shortstop, lined his first pitch straight to the Salem first baseman for the third out, the Big Reds scrambled out of the dugout for the top of the seventh, out in front by a run.

Chip walked slowly toward the mound. Then he heard them again, heard them jeering the Rock. The loud, raucous voices were bitter, persistent, and familiar.

"You're just plain lucky, loser!"

"Rockwell, why don't you quit while you're still breathing?"

"Yeah, Grandpa, retire right now! Give some young guy a chance!"

"You're a has-been, Rockwell! Just a has-been!"

Chip stopped abruptly and turned to look at the six or seven men in their early to mid-twenties who'd been razzing and taunting Rockwell all through the game. He knew each one well.

"Hey, look at Rockwell's pet! He's mad at us!"

"What you lookin' at, Hilton? Get out on the mound and quit posing for the fans. We'll be rid of you, too, in another three weeks!"

"Yeah, grandstander, don't look so tough. Your mommy wouldn't like it!"

"No, nor Granddaddy Rockwell either!"

"Hilton, you and Rockwell are two of a kind."

"Yeah, two Valley Falls has-beens!"

The crowd in the stands started taking sides. A few joined the hecklers in attacking Rockwell and Hilton, but it was obvious the vast majority disapproved of the poor sportsmanship of the loudmouthed group. The whole field was in an uproar.

Carl Carey walked out from behind the plate thumping the ball in his catcher's glove as Speed Morris, Chris Badger, Cody Collins, and Biggie Cohen came trotting up to join Chip. Cohen grasped Hilton by the arm. "Come on, Chip, keep your head in the game. Let's put 'em away!"

"Yeah, Chip, don't let 'em razz you!"

The roar grew louder as Rockwell leaped from the dugout and walked quickly toward the group of players on the baseline. "Forget it, Chip," he said quietly. "Finish the game. That's all that matters." He gestured toward the stands. "They mean nothing."

Rockwell grasped Chip by both arms and firmly eased him around to face the diamond. He slapped the tall youngster gently on the back and gave him a little push toward the pitcher's mound.

"Play ball!"

The plate umpire, mask in hand, broke up the little group of players, and the mood of the crowd changed almost instantly. "Play ball," came booming from the stands. "Play ball!"

Chip was seething as he completed his warm-up pitches. This had been going on all spring. Game after game, at home or away, this same group of hecklers had plagued Rockwell and the team until it had become almost unbearable.

Directly behind the plate, in the grandstand, a small bronze-faced man sat quietly listening to the yells, cheers, catcalls, and general crowd-conversation during the commotion. Now he again concentrated on the lanky, blond kid out on the mound. He heard what was being said, but he was chiefly interested in the young pitcher's reaction to the crowd baiting.

"Don't know why they're riding Hilton," someone said. "He's won every game he's pitched!"

"Yeah, and leads the team in hitting too!"

"Best pitcher in the state!" a booming voice asserted.

"Ready for the big leagues right now!" someone added.

The bronze-faced man turned to the fan sitting next to him. "Are those men with the other team?" he asked, nodding toward the noisy group who had been riding Rockwell.

"Them?" his seatmate asked, glancing at the hecklers. "No, they're from Valley Falls, but they hate Rockwell! He's the coach, you know." He nodded toward the loudmouthed bleacher bums again. "That group has been after Rockwell for two years. They desperately want him to quit so they can get one of their own crowd in at the school as the coach."

"That's funny," the stranger said dryly. "The guy gives them a state championship team in three sports and they want him ditched! Don't get it!"

"Well, it's a long story. Rock's sorta independent and runs a good, clean program. Some of the alumni want to control the coaches and their teams, but Rockwell won't hold still for it. Don't blame him! Anyway, they resent the way the coach ignores 'em, and now it's a regular feud.

"The red-faced one is Jerry Davis. His father owns the big jewelry store in town, and Jerry thinks and acts like he runs the business and most of Valley Falls too. Never played sports but thinks he knows more than everybody.

"Muddy Waters and Dick Cantwell, sitting next to him, aren't such bad guys, but they hang around with Davis, and he's got them under his thumb. They do just about whatever Jerry wants them to do.

"The two tough-looking ones on the end are Buck Adams and Peck Weaver—locals always in some kind of trouble."

The conversation stopped when Salem's first hitter of the big end of their batting order tapped the plate with his bat and the slender teenager on the mound toed the rubber. Chip was still burning with anger, but it wasn't apparent in his pitching. He mowed the Salem hitters down one-two-three, turned abruptly as he delivered the last strike, and headed for Ohlsen Stadium and the locker room in the high school building just beyond. Trooping after him came his teammates and little Paddy Jackson, the bat boy, trotting along with Chip's warm-up jacket.

Bringing up the rear, the two game umpires walked slowly along talking about the game and Coach Henry Rockwell.

"He's sure strong, isn't he?"

"Rock? Sure! Just as much fight as ever!"

His companion laughed. "You can say that again! Hasn't changed in the last twenty years, far as I can see!"

"They really ganged up on Rockwell. I didn't like it!"

"Hear they're trying to force the school board to retire him!"

"*Force* is right! He won't quit! Ain't built that way! This whole place wouldn't be the same without him. They don't know what they've got."

The last person to leave the grandstand was the tanned stranger. He walked leisurely along the wide wooden grandstands and down the broad steps to the concrete walk leading to the street. He'd enjoyed the game for several reasons. The number one reason was the sensational all-around play of a young high school pitcher by the name of William "Chip" Hilton. The tall, slender teenager was three weeks away from graduation, and Stu Gardner might have been his shadow, the way he followed every move Chip made.

The other reason for Gardner's enjoyment of the game was another Valley Falls High School senior who knew just how to play first base. Benjamin "Biggie" Cohen was six feet four inches, left-handed, and possessed a strong arm. Quick and agile, Biggie was a master of the shift and the stretch, as well as the pickup. The bulky athlete was an ideal first baseman. Gardner had worried a bit about the 230 pounds Cohen carried, but Biggie was as strong as a bull and there wasn't an ounce of fat on his body. The agile first baseman was a good competitor too. He hit the long ball, and Stu had him tabbed as a surefire, big-league prospect.

Stewart "Stu" Gardner had been in organized baseball a long time, first as a player, later as manager of a Triple A class club, and now as a scout for a major league club. It was his job to discover talent. Gardner had been watching the Valley Falls Big Reds for the past month and had put aside his other prospects for the time being. Right here in Valley Falls he'd discovered two athletes

BLEACHER BUMS

who would make his job secure for years to come if they were as good as they'd looked in the past few games.

Gardner was thorough. In his scouting, he charted each prospect's emotional stability as thoroughly as his physical ability. The veteran scout was certain both youngsters possessed plenty of baseball ability, but it's tough to gauge emotional toughness from the stands; he really had to know a player to judge him on that score. He'd been interested in Hilton's reaction to the razzing because he'd known a lot of fine ballplayers who might have enjoyed a successful big-league career if only they'd possessed self-control.

A big-league scout isn't paid just to travel around the country watching games and players; he's got to deliver, got to turn up a real ballplayer every so often. Stu Gardner was past due, way past due. Now, as he sauntered along behind the crowd, he breathed a fervent prayer that the kids he'd been watching possessed mental discipline—and that he'd be the only big-league scout to see Chip Hilton and Biggie Cohen play baseball before graduation. In only three weeks, they'd end their high school careers and become eligible to sign a contract. He hoped it was with the Drakes.

CHAPTER 2

Diamond Politics

CHIP HILTON hadn't spoken a word since he'd pivoted
and started for the locker room after the third strike on
the last Salem batter. Leaning back against his locker,
relaxing from that after-game tiredness that often hits
an athlete so suddenly, he tried to get the anger out of his
heart. The riding he'd taken today was just about the last
straw. He could only take so much.

The Big Reds' small squad was composed of two groups:
one from the South Side and one from the West Side. The
West Side was represented by most of the members of what
was jokingly called the Hilton Athletic Club or the Hilton A.
C. The Hilton home was the "club's headquarters"; the members were Chip's closest friends, and most of them played on
the Valley Falls varsity squad. They included Speed Morris,
shortstop; Biggie Cohen, first base; Soapy Smith, catcher,
pitcher, and outfielder; and Red Schwartz, outfielder.

The South Siders were Chris Badger, stocky, heavy-
set third baseman; Nick Trullo, husky southpaw; Carl

DIAMOND POLITICS

Carey, a fighting catcher who shared the receiving with Soapy Smith; and Cody Collins, peppery second baseman and chief "talk it up" player on the team.

These two groups, formerly long-standing rivals, had been brought together through the efforts of Chip Hilton over the last two years. Then, appreciating the athletic potential of the two groups, Rockwell had cleverly substituted team spirit in place of neighborhood competition. Along the way, he'd gained the respect and loyalty of both groups. Now the cowardly attacks by Rockwell's enemies had welded the team into a fighting squad, each athlete willing and eager to play his heart out to help his coach.

Every sports fan in town knew Rockwell's enemies had been waging a relentless campaign to force the veteran mentor to accept retirement. A few of these realized that retirement meant the end to the one thing in the world the veteran coach liked best: coaching the students at Valley Falls. Every ballplayer on Valley Falls's state championship team knew how Rockwell felt, and each one wished he could do something about it.

After the game with Salem, Rockwell and his assistant, Chet Stewart, had remained behind to help gather up the ball bag, the bats, and the bases and to help Taps Browning, the manager, carry the usual assortment of equipment to the gym. After a last check to see that nothing had been overlooked, the two coaches and the manager trudged slowly along behind the umpires and were the last to reach the locker room.

Rockwell's stocky figure was clothed in an old, faded tight-fitting baseball uniform that seemed molded to his body. The clack-clack, clackety-clack of his spikes rang out sharply and warned the Big Reds of his approach, but they didn't look up when he came clattering into the locker room. Just inside the door, Rockwell paused and his eyes swept the room from one boy to another. He sensed the kids were bitter over the riding he and Chip had taken, and he decided right then and there to get the resentment out of their heads. The quicker the better!

This team stood in grave danger of coming apart at the seams. Not because of conditioning, injuries, or lack of ability, but because of emotional stress. He'd seen it coming ever since Davis and his parasites had started their bitter riding campaign at the very first game. He'd fix that! Right now! He'd get their minds off that problem! He'd do a little riding himself!

Rockwell had a good weapon. The annual elections would be held shortly to choose members of the senior class to take over a one-day administration of the municipal government of Valley Falls. The ball club members had talked of little else during the past two weeks. Rockwell would ride them about that distraction.

The Big Reds knew Rockwell's moods, and his first words warned the team that he was angry.

"That was a fine exhibition," he stormed.

"You must have been reading last year's press clippings! You're sure not playing like last year's ball club!

"If it isn't asking too much, I'd like to request more concentration on defending the state baseball championship and less on the school political campaigns!"

Rockwell's sharp black eyes darted from one player to another. The kids were startled. Good! He had them going!

"Another thing," he snapped. "I don't want to hear any more talk about being stale!" He paused to let that sink in and then continued, biting off his words sharply.

"You have to be good to go stale! Now beat it! And show up here tomorrow thinking baseball, playing baseball, and looking like baseball players—not like Valley Falls politicians! That's all!"

A little later Chip, Soapy Smith, Biggie Cohen, Red Schwartz, and Taps Browning piled into Speed Morris's red fastback Mustang and started home. There was an absence of the usual bickering, jibes, and needling. Everyone seemed subdued—except Soapy. He leaned forward and tapped Speed on the shoulder.

"This crate's on its last legs, my friend. Something doesn't sound right," he warned. "Ya know, they shoot horses—even Mustangs—to put them out of their misery."

"Yeah, we know all about it," Biggie said menacingly, "but you just better be quiet about it—"

Then, just as Soapy had predicted, the tired old three-speed burped, chuckled a few times as if anticipating coming events, and stopped dead.

"You and your big mouth," Biggie growled. "Why don't you keep it shut?"

Soapy nodded grimly. "Yeah," he agreed, "why don't I?"

Speed raised the hood. "Hmm . . . It's an engine. Looks just the same," he said dryly.

"Yeah," Soapy nodded, "just the same as it did thirty years ago! Except it worked then! Well, Speed, you're supposed to be the mechanic. Show us how good you are. Hah! This I gotta see!"

Biggie glared at Soapy over Speed's shoulder, and for the next fifteen minutes Soapy was quiet. Then he couldn't stand it any longer.

"It's tired," he said wearily, "tired like me. Well," he gasped, "we gotta go get someone to tow us."

"No way," Schwartz grunted. "That takes too long, and I wanna go home. C'mon guys," he said. "Come on, let's see if we can get it going with a push. If we can make it to the top of the hill, we'll be OK."

Digging in, they puffed and pushed but made little progress up the steep grade. Soapy pushed, too, but he kept looking over his shoulder for someone to rescue them. Eventually a car did come along, a car with SHERIFF painted on the side.

"It's Sheriff Birks's car, and Early's driving," Soapy yelled hopefully. "Hey, Early, give us a tow, will ya?"

The cruiser slowed down, and Early Birks, a member of their class and the sheriff's son, leaned out to get a better view. "What's up?" he yelled, grinning delightedly. "Havin' trouble, guys? Looks like good exercise! See ya tomorrow! Take it easy, Soapy!" The car shot forward and up over the hill, a derisive, "Heyuh, heyuh, heyuh" echoing in its wake.

"Wow, he's a real squirrel, isn't he?" Soapy laughed.

"That's why they call him 'Squirrely Early,'" Red cracked.

"Soapy, you oughta kept your big mouth shut," Biggie growled. "What's the matter with you—laying us open for a nut like that? Why ask him?"

"Who wants to keep pushing?"

"I'd rather push this thing every day than ask Early Birks for a favor."

"What d'ya mean *favor?*" Soapy demanded. "It's a town car, ain't it? We got as much right to use that car as Early has, ain't we? Town cars are s'ported by taxes, ain't they? And our parents pay the city bills, don't they? We got more right to use that car than Early Birks has!"

"How you figure?" Speed demanded.

Soapy grunted. "Easy! There's more of us!"

Schwartz laughed. "You'd get a long way in this town with that philosophy," he said.

"Yeah, why not?" Soapy demanded. "You tell me why not?"

Speed laughed. "Because Mayor Condon, Bill Cowles, and Sheriff Birks have this town locked up," he said. "That's why!"

Soapy was belligerent. "What d'ya mean, locked up?"

"You know what he means," Schwartz said sourly. "He means those three guys run the town! Anything they want to do—they do!"

"Why don't we change things?" Soapy persisted. "Answer me that! Maybe we could, if we could vote!" he beamed. "Soon as we can vote, we'll throw 'em out!"

"Take more than a few votes to throw them out," Biggie said slowly. "They're organized! You know," he continued softly, "I like that Early less and less every day. He and his crew are trying to run things at school just like his old man and *his* crowd run the town. Look at the school elections. You know how the senior class votes each year for students to "govern" Valley Falls for a day? Well, Early's running for county sheriff like his dad, and Russ Cowles wants to be the chief of police just like *his* father.

"Right!" Soapy interrupted. "And Mark Condon wants to keep the mayor stuff in the family! And you know what? He'll do it!"

"He won't if I can do anything about it," Biggie drawled. "Maybe we oughta draw up a platform and elect some regular guys—"

"Hey!" Soapy shouted. "I've got a brainstorm. Let's put Chip forward for mayor. He'll win in a snap!"

Red Schwartz was enthusiastic. "Atta baby, Soapy," he cried. "It's a lock! What d'ya say, Chip?"

"No, thanks," Chip said firmly. "I'm into enough things now. We've got all we can do to defend the state championship," he said quietly. "Look, I don't want to get mixed up in that student election stuff. We've got plenty to do until graduation, like classes, final exams, and playing ball. Remember what Rock said. Let's skip it!"

"I sure hate to see that crowd get in," Schwartz grumbled. "They already lord it over the student council, the student court, and everything else. You know what'll happen just as well as I do! Mark Condon will head up the Citizens Party and run for mayor; Russ Cowles will run for chief of police; Squirrely Early Birks will be the candidate for sheriff; and the rest of their crowd will be appointed to the town council. I can see 'em right now! It's only for a day, but they'll make it a real long miserable day!"

"Not if Chip runs," Speed said. "Chip would win easy!"

"Right," Soapy added. "You run, Chip, and I bet you a million bucks you win!"

"It's too bad Mayor Stanton and Sheriff Brock lost the elections last year. Dad said they were good, fair leaders," Speed said resignedly, rubbing engine grime on his jeans.

"Well, the people elected them," Schwartz said. "They asked for it!"

"Uh-huh," Biggie grunted, "and they got Condon and Birks."

"They got more than that," Schwartz added. "They got old man Davis, Cantwell, and Frank Greer on the school board, and Bill Cowles for chief of police."

"There're some good people on the board," Chip said. "J. P. Ohlsen's a member, and Mr. Stanton and Mrs. Thomas."

"If they're so good," Soapy objected, "why don't they do something about Condon, Cowles, and Birks and the rest of them?"

"Because they're the Board of Education and not city council members," Biggie explained patiently. "Don't you

understand? The school board and the council are separate. Of course, Mayor Condon sits in on all the school
board meetings and acts like an advisor or something.
It's not as separate as it should be, at least that's what
my dad says. He says there are only two or three good
members on the school board. The others, the majority,
are all Condon's followers."

Red Schwartz was getting worked up. "Wonder how
many people in town know about all the fishing trips
taken in the city cars, and the way Cowles overlooks
Adams's and Weaver's gambling over on the South Side,
and the new walk and driveway at Mayor Condon's
house put in by city workers. And . . . aw, what's the use?"

Speed took over. "How about all the materials and
labor? Who paid for that?" he demanded.

"You can bet Condon didn't!" Biggie said dryly.

"Ya know," Soapy gravely informed his friends, "my
Dad's always rantin' about the high tax rates, and I'm
beginnin' to see the light!"

"You'll see a light, all right," Biggie rumbled, "and
hear a little bell tinkling, too, if you ask any more favors
from Early Birks."

Soapy started to say something, but catching the
glare in Biggie's eyes, he moved to the back of the car and
cautiously put his hands on the bumper. "C'mon guys,"
he said, "let's go. I gotta be at work by seven o'clock."

While the charter members of the Hilton A. C. were
having car trouble, Jerry Davis, Muddy Waters, and Dick
Cantwell were rolling along in Davis's Cadillac.

"You gotta hand it to that kid," Waters said grudg-
ingly. "He's got talent!"

Jerry Davis nodded. "He's good all right, if you like
that kind."

"Boy, he was burning today," Cantwell chuckled. "I thought for a minute he was coming right up into the stands."

Davis grinned. "Weaver and Adams sure had him going. They hate his guts!"

"Why shouldn't they?" Waters asked dryly. "Didn't Weaver start a fight that Hilton finished over on the hill last year, right in front of the whole South Side? Sure he and Adams hate Hilton's guts! But Hilton taught them a few lessons."

"Hold everything," Davis said softly. "I've got an idea. A good idea!"

"What?" Waters asked.

"Something good! You know how Zimmerman won't tolerate fighting? Well, why not maneuver Hilton into a fight with Adams or Weaver at one of the games?"

"What for?"

"What for? Nothing much, 'cept Zimmerman will suspend Hilton and we'll have Rockwell right where we want him! Get it?"

"No."

Davis made a gesture of exasperation. "Trullo's the only other pitcher, isn't he? And you know how Rockwell is—he won't use a kid more than every three or four days. That'll leave only one pitcher!"

"Now I get it! Then they'll start to lose."

"Right! And since everyone in town thinks the team's a cinch to repeat the championship—"

"You mean they'll blame Rockwell!"

"You know how the people are in this town. They can't stand to lose. Once they start to lose, they'll pressure the school board, and it will be good-bye Rockwell. Then we'll be on top and in control—and rid of the old goat for good!"

CHAPTER 3

Make a Difference

VALLEY FALLS High School normally would have been buzzing about the previous victory and the pitching duel between Rick Parcels and Chip Hilton—but not this Friday morning. Between classes, in every hallway and classroom, student politicians promoted their various candidates for the senior elections. At lunchtime, the broad stone steps leading to the main entrance, as well as the gym terrace in the rear, were thronged with students discussing the party platforms and the possible candidates.

That afternoon Mr. Zimmerman called a special election assembly for the high school. Mayor Condon and several members of the town council were seated on the stage. After the jazz band completed a short musical program, each council member spoke briefly.

Principal Zimmerman then extolled the virtues of "our great mayor," after which Condon took center stage. The town's top executive greeted the students warmly and advised them that he and his entire administration were looking forward to Friday, May 18, when the town government would be turned over for the day to the successful student electees. He promised the full cooperation of each city administrator and said every office would be prepared for the "invasion." Although a bit patronizing, Mayor Condon attempted to be humorous as he spoke of the enthusiasm with which the members of the city government were "engraving keys to the city for their student successors on Friday, May 18."

While Mayor Condon was talking, Chip was absent-mindedly flipping through the *Yellow Jacket,* the student newspaper. One of the editors had researched some old, outdated laws—known initially as blue laws—that no one paid attention to but were still on the books in many cities across the country. Most of them were pretty funny. One read: "In Kansas City, Missouri, only married women and girls over seventeen can wear lipstick."

Chip smiled at a sudden thought: *Someone could have lots of fun if he got elected and then enforced all the old blue laws.* "Hey," he muttered to himself, "that's an idea!" Then Chip had a more serious thought: *A person could really accomplish something on Friday, May 18, if the mayor was sincere in what he said—and if the right crowd was behind him.*

The germ of an idea began to develop in Chip's mind. *Maybe a guy could make a difference—even if only for a day.* Then he sighed. *Better skip it . . . better concentrate on school and baseball.* He probably wouldn't be elected even if he became a candidate.

In spite of himself, however, his thoughts jumped back to the previous evening in the Sugar Bowl. Chip's friends had again urged him to let them nominate him for mayor.

"Aw, c'mon, Chip," Soapy had pleaded. "You'd win. It's a no-brainer. You could be the mayor and Biggie could be the chief of police, an' . . . an' . . . I could be the city auditor. Then I could count all the money and find out where it's all goin'. What d'ya say? Nobody likes Early Birks and those guys. They just elect them 'cause nobody else runs. What d'ya say?"

Chip had been adamant in his decision. He told them he didn't have time, not with school and work and baseball.

Speed, Biggie, Red, and Taps Browning had joined Soapy in pressuring Chip, but without success. Petey Jackson jumped in, too, and just about summarized everyone's arguments when he said, "C'mon, Chip. Have some fun. All you do is work all the time. You're too serious!"

But Chip had remained firm, and his friends had finally given up. Now, for a brief moment, Chip was sorry he'd been so determined. It could have been fun . . . .

Just before the end of the assembly, Mr. Zimmerman announced that the Home Rule Party nominations would be held at a three o'clock assembly on May 2, and the Citizens Party nominations would be on the following day at two o'clock. The elections would be held on Wednesday, May 9, with the polls open from one o'clock to three o'clock in the gym. He promised the results would be announced late that afternoon before the end of the Parkton game.

Rockwell liked his ballplayers to be able to play more than one position. One of his favorite strategies was to insist that all catchers and pitchers shag flies as a conditioner. This year, practice for the pitchers and catchers was extremely important because it was necessary for him to use one of his batteries in the outfield every game.

Coach Rockwell had been handicapped the year before with a small squad, but he had still nursed the team through to win the state championship. That feat had been nothing compared to the task facing him this year. His outfield was patrolled by only one regular, Red Schwartz, in center field. Since no new candidate had shown up, Rockwell had been forced to use one of his catchers, Carl Carey or Soapy Smith, and one of his pitchers, Chip Hilton or Nick Trullo, in the other outfield spots.

The only other player available was little Lefty Peters who'd been used as a pitcher the year before until his appendicitis attack, which had required an emergency operation. Lefty was back but had never fully recovered, and Rockwell had never used him on the hill and only once or twice in the outfield.

Chip Hilton was a ballplayer's ballplayer—a hard, consistent hitter who could pull in flies, throw with the best of them, and field his pitching position flawlessly. But there, Rockwell's good fortune ended. Soapy Smith and Nick Trullo were both equipped with strong throwing arms but were uncertain fielders. Carl Carey and Lefty Peters seemed unable to judge fly balls, and neither had strong throwing arms to handle the long throws, particularly from right field to third base.

Rockwell assigned Friday afternoon's infield practice to his assistant, Chet Stewart, and personally spent the whole practice session with the outfield. Time after time he lifted high flies, long, low drives, and an occasional hard grass cutter to Chip, Lefty, Nick, Carl, Soapy, and Red. After two hours of this grinding practice, Rockwell grunted and sent them on three laps around the field and to the showers.

Petey Jackson, Valley Falls's self-proclaimed sports guru and Sugar Bowl manager, was taking advantage of the late afternoon break in business to read a copy of the

MAKE A DIFFERENCE

Yellow Jacket. Petey was interested in anything that concerned the Big Reds and Valley Falls High School. Although a number of years younger, Chip Hilton was one of Petey's heroes, and the two had worked at the Sugar Bowl for several years. The previous summer Soapy Smith had been added to the staff, and the three friends made up a happy working combination for John Schroeder's Sugar Bowl.

Petey read the *Yellow Jacket* aloud, mumbling the words faster and faster as he read about the coming elections and the possible candidates. "Same old crowd," he muttered, "same old crowd. Trying to run everything— Early Birks, Russ Cowles, Mark Condon, and that bunch." Petey snorted and threw the paper over his shoulder. Then he picked up the latest edition of the *Times*. Turning to the sports page, he focused on the "Times and Sports" article. Halfway through the column Petey mumbled, "He's at it again. What is the matter with that guy?"

Times and Sports
by Muddy Waters

Valley Falls High School may be the defending diamond champions of the state, but the Big Reds will be in the stands watching this year's championship games at State on May 23, 25, and 26. Why?

Because Rockwell has only two hurlers, and both are overworked . . . Because prima donna Chip Hilton is showing his poor attitude and can't take a little harmless razzing from loyal bleacher fans . . . Because the Big Reds have won or lost every game so far by a single run. . . . Because Biggie Cohen is the only starter hitting consistently . . . Because sixteen runs and twenty-nine hits in seven games against the weakest teams in Section Two indicate an absence of power . . .

Finally, because Henry Rockwell has overtrained the squad and is trying to teach high school kids big-league baseball.

Petey couldn't take anymore. He slammed the paper down on the marble counter and loudly expressed his opinion of a certain sports columnist. Right then and there he decided that come tomorrow afternoon his grandmother was going to be "dangerously ill" again, and he personally was going to check up on the Big Reds' baseball team.

Petey figured he'd need full cooperation from his grandmother because Saturday afternoons were busy at the Sugar Bowl, and John Schroeder might check up on him—or worse, send Doc Jones on a house call to a very healthy Grandma Jackson. So that night Petey didn't stop but hurried right past Sorelli's, carrying a nice box of candy and a large bouquet of flowers.

The next morning John Schroeder was unusually kind when Petey referred to his grandmother's sudden illness. "Of course," he insisted, when Petey demurred feebly. "Of course you're going home! We'll work it out! Everybody will be at the game anyway!"

Chip and Soapy were deeply concerned about Petey's grandmother too.

"What's the matter with her?" Chip asked.

Petey sighed dramatically. "It's spells she gets, Chip. They just come—sudden-like, of course—"

"What kind of spells?" Soapy asked solicitously.

"Well, it's a kind of a sugar reaction," Petey explained uncertainly. "You've heard of that?"

Soapy nodded. "Oh, sure! I know about that."

"Is there anything we can do?" Chip asked anxiously.

"No," Petey said sadly, "there's nothing much anyone can do. She'll snap out of it tomorrow."

"We'll stop by and see her," Soapy said consolingly, "on our way to the game."

"Oh, no," Petey cried hastily, "don't do that. You might upset her."

"You sure?"

Petey was sure, and at twelve o'clock he hurried home to make sure about that and to figure out another problem.

John Schroeder and Doc Jones were avid sports fans. The two old friends were strong believers in the value of high school athletics. When Henry Rockwell's Big Reds played a game, any kind of game, the two were sure to be on hand.

As in most small towns, Saturday afternoon was a shopping and business day in Valley Falls. Doc Jones maintained morning office hours but eliminated office hours on Saturday afternoons. Some residents wondered why John Schroeder wasn't on the job at his Sugar Bowl on busy Saturday afternoons. That is, of course, unless they knew John Schroeder, knew that he was financially secure, that business—like athletics—was a hobby, and that he was keenly interested in the sports achievements of one of his employees.

Chip Hilton had worked at John Schroeder's Sugar Bowl for several years. Schroeder was extremely fond of the teenager and had arranged Chip's working hours so they wouldn't interfere with his schoolwork or athletics. Chip was extremely grateful for John Schroeder's kindness, and he'd earned his employer's deepest respect because he never shirked his responsibilities.

PITCHERS' DUEL

Compared to the bleachers, baseball's grandstand seats fill slowly. But if all grandstand fans were as fervent as John Schroeder and Doc Jones, the reverse would have been true. The two Big Red fans liked to watch the pregame hitting, fielding, and warm-up practice almost as much as the game. This afternoon they were the first to arrive, eagerly hurrying to their favorite seats, right behind the plate and high up in the grandstand.

"What a day, what a day," Doc gasped enthusiastically as he puffed along behind John Schroeder. "Makes a man feel almost like living."

The doctor was as correct in his meteorological observation as the weather channel. It was perfect baseball weather—late spring with a hint of the hot summer days to come in the soft, warm breeze, scented by the freshly mowed outfield.

The Big Reds had finished their hitting practice. Now the sharp crack of Delford's bats resounded in the tight little park and brought scattered cheers from the bleachers behind the visitors' dugout. The bleachers extended from the small grandstand parallel with the foul lines. Today, both sides were fairly well filled.

John Schroeder and Doc Jones were the first seated in the grandstand, but the first bleacher fans to arrive were Buck Adams, Peck Weaver, and three or four of their followers. They had arrived early and were spread out in the front row of the bleachers on the first base side of the field, right above the Valley Falls dugout. Today, however, they were unusually quiet.

Chip, leisurely limbering up with Carl Carey in front of the dugout, acted as if he hadn't noticed the arrival of the hecklers, but he was puzzled. *They're too quiet. It's too good to be true,* he mused. *They're up to something.*

CHAPTER 4

Candidate for Mayor

NICK TRULLO started for the Big Reds with Soapy Smith behind the plate. While the big southpaw was warming up, someone behind the dugout started an argument with another spectator. Chip, almost at their feet under the shelter of the dugout roof, could hear the hecklers as clearly as if he'd been right in the middle of them. Rockwell, he noted with a quick side glance, seemed completely oblivious to the heated conversation.

"Rockwell's all washed up! Hasn't kept up with the times!"

"Times or no times, he keeps winning—"

"How you figure that? Look what happened last fall in football! Had a veteran squad! Same team that won the state championship the year before! How about that?"

"Yes, but he was sick! Wasn't with the team most of the season. They finished strong when he got back! Knocked off Steeltown, the state champs! Is that bad?"

PITCHERS' DUEL

"How about basketball? Didn't lose a man from the team that won the championship the year before! How d'ya explain that?"

"Would've gone to the tournament if it hadn't been for a snowstorm—and if a ball hadn't deflated in the air and cost the kids the game! Can't blame Rockwell for an 'act of God' or a freak accident, can you?"

"Aw, that game shouldn't have even been close. He's through, I'm telling you, through! Look, you don't mean to say you approve of him keeping some up-and-coming young coach out of a job, do you?"

"Well, maybe I do and maybe I don't! Can't see as how that's got anything to do with coaching, though—"

A sudden burst of cheers from the Delford bleachers and an answering roar from the Big Reds' supporters drowned out the argument. The game was on.

Like many lefties, Nick Trullo was wild and fast, a combination that smothers most hitters. But Delford waited him out, and it paid off. Nick walked the first three batters, struck out the cleanup man, and then walked in the first run of the game. Before the side was retired, Delford had scored three runs.

Trullo's wildness seemed to affect his teammates; they couldn't do anything right. At bat, they hit straight at the fielders for easy outs, and in the field, nothing clicked. In the bottom half of the fifth, the Big Reds were trailing 8-0. Weaver and Adams suddenly came to life with a vicious attack on Rockwell, but most of it was lost in the crowd's tumult.

Rockwell and Stewart, along with Pop Brown—the team's trainer—and little Paddy, Chip, Carl, and all the Big Reds were in front of the dugout pleading with Cody Collins to "start the fire" and for the Big Reds to "go get some runs!"

As Cody pounded the plate with his bat, Rockwell started down the dugout steps. Peck Weaver suddenly leaned over the low roof and threw a styrofoam cup filled with hot coffee directly in the unsuspecting coach's face. It was done so quickly and cleverly that few, if any, spectators saw what happened.

Chip, so close behind Rockwell that some of the liquid splattered into his eyes, did see Weaver commit the act. Without thinking, Chip dashed around the dugout, vaulted the low railing, and was on top of Weaver almost before anyone else could move. Anyone else, that is, except a slender, bearded man wearing sunglasses and a comical, oversized hat with its brim turned down all around his face. The stranger moved with unusual speed as he joined Chip. Although several people recalled the incident later and wondered who the man was, his identity was no mystery to two men who'd had a good view of the incident from their vantage point high in the grandstand.

Soapy, Carl, Speed, Biggie, and Nick were right behind the bearded stranger, over the rail and into the melee. It took the combined efforts of Rockwell, Chet Stewart, Principal Zimmerman, and big Bob Gilbert, the only police officer present, to get the thoroughly enraged players back down on the field again.

All over the park, in the bleachers, and in the grandstand the fans were standing on tiptoe trying to get a good view of the action.

"What happened?"

"What's going on?"

"Look at Rockwell's face and uniform!"

"Looks like someone started something he couldn't finish!"

Chip followed his teammates back on the field, still boiling, but feeling a bit of satisfaction because he'd given Peck

Weaver what he'd deserved. But he wasn't prepared for the principal's descent from the stands. Carl Zimmerman went straight for Chip, anger written all over his face.

"That was a disgraceful exhibition, Hilton," he said heatedly. "You're suspended from baseball and from Valley Falls High School as of this minute! Leave the field immediately, and see me in my office Tuesday at eleven o'clock." Zimmerman turned on his heel and returned to the grandstand.

"But, Zim," Rockwell remonstrated, following along behind the principal, "we're playing Stratford Monday, and Chip's got to work that game—"

Zimmerman's blue eyes were hard and unyielding as he faced Rockwell. "Hilton is suspended, Hank," he said firmly, "from baseball and from school." He turned away and again started for the stands.

Rockwell kept pace with the irate school administrator, talking earnestly. "They started it, Zim. It wasn't Chip's fault—"

Zimmerman paused once more. "I saw the whole thing, Hank. A player should be able to take a little good-natured joshing from the spectators. Hilton lost his head. A captain is supposed to set a good example for his team. I won't discuss it further until Tuesday."

"Good-natured joshing?" Rockwell fumed. "If that's your idea of fun, one of us is out of his mind!"

But Rockwell was talking to himself and the empty air.

He was still talking to himself as he trudged past the scoreboard with his arms full of baseball equipment.

"Whitewashed," he muttered, "shut out ten to nothing! And who's going to work Monday? This could ruin our whole season!"

The local fans were low in spirits as they made their way out of the stands—all except John Schroeder and Doc

Jones. They attracted angry stares by bursting into long laughter from time to time. However, as soon as they noted the shocked expressions on the faces of nearby fans, they subsided into low chuckles and subdued tones.

"When did you first recognize Petey?" Jones asked. Schroeder chuckled again. "Oh, long before the game started. Of course, when he went to Chip's aid there was no doubt about it."

Doc Jones wiped a laughing tear from his eye. "I can still see him holding his beard with one hand and flailing away at Adams with the other!"

"You know, Doc, poor Petey's clueless. He actually thinks he's pulled a fast one on me with his sick grandma routine. Next time, let's bring Grandma Jackson along. She can carry her pretty flowers, sit between us, and we'll both help her eat her candy! Wouldn't you just love to see Petey's face? You bring the camera." The two old friends were still chuckling half an hour later when they arrived at the Sugar Bowl.

The gloom hung like a thick curtain over the whole place, but it was heaviest near the fountain. Soapy was all alone and feeling down. He had tried to talk to Chip with no success. Chip wasn't talking then, and he wasn't saying much the next morning when his mom joined him in the family room. Chip, on his stomach, was playing with Hoops on the carpet. Time and again, the big tomcat twitched his tail and then lunged for Chip's outstretched fingers. After several attempts to stir Chip out of his lethargy, his mom went directly to the heart of his problem.

"Don't worry about it, Chip," Mary Hilton said soothingly. "You defended your coach and that's laudable. Everything will come out all right. You'll see Tuesday. Just tell him the whole story."

"But, Mom, what can I say?"

"If you made a mistake, son, be responsible and say so—"

"I can't say that, Mom. I don't feel that way. I'm not a bit sorry. I'd do it again! I was defending Coach Rockwell."

"If you're sure your actions were justified, Chip, then there's nothing to fear. I'm sure Mr. Zimmerman appreciates the truth and will allow for your honest convictions. Like you, your dad always tried to do the right thing and everybody respected him. But he didn't approve of fighting as a solution."

A little later Chip left the room carrying the sports section of the *Times*. He didn't want his mom to see Muddy Waters's column, then or ever.

But Chip hadn't counted on Karen Browning, their next door neighbor and his mom's good friend. Coming home from church that morning, Suzy and Taps's mom tried to lift some of the sadness from Mary Hilton's heart.

"Everything will come out all right, Mary," Karen said softly. "No one pays any attention to that Waters."

"Waters?" Mary Hilton echoed. "What are you talking about, Karen?"

Standing at the Brownings' kitchen counter, Mary Hilton found out what her friend meant. She read Waters's article with mounting indignation and amazement. Her gentle nature was incapable of understanding the motive behind such a story. In spite of her reaction to the column, however, her heart filled with warmth at yet another instance of her son's mature thoughtfulness. *So that's why I couldn't find the sports page this morning. . . .*

After lunch, Chip studied until Soapy, Biggie, Speed, and Red showed up. They were gloomy and discouraged, still stinging from the Delford defeat. They also bitterly criticized Principal Zimmerman.

CANDIDATE FOR MAYOR

Soapy, naturally, was the most outspoken. "What kind of a deal is this? What's the matter with that Zimmerman?" he demanded. "I'm going to go see him and give him a piece of my mind!"

Biggie laughed, "Soapy, make it a little piece; you don't have much to spare."

"Hey," Soapy bounced back, "that's the first game he's seen all year, and he gets on us instead of Weaver and his bozo stooges. What we gonna do tomorrow? Who's gonna throw?"

No one knew the answer to Soapy's questions, and the friends lapsed into a deep silence that was only broken when, a little later, Petey and Paddy Jackson arrived.

Petey reported that his grandmother was much, much better. In fact, she was doing great, up and around—even eating candy!

"Guess what?" he asked, after an awkward pause. "Guess who I saw last night at Sor—" Petey tried to stop the last words, but it was too late.

"Last night?" his listeners chorused.

The silence that followed was heavy. Petey was thinking furiously as he hedged. "I . . . er . . . that is . . . I stopped by Sorelli's poolroom after I found Grandma was so improved, and who do you think I saw?"

Petey waited expectantly, but there was no response.

"Well, Weaver was there." Petey shot a quick glance at Chip and continued. "Weaver was there with a black eye, and Adams; and who do you think they were talking to? Jerry Davis and Muddy Waters!"

"So what?" Soapy demanded.

"So what?" Petey echoed. "Nothing, except I heard Davis and Waters laughing about Chip falling for Weaver's trick. All of them were talking about Chip falling into the trap! Only Weaver and Adams didn't do any laughing. You know something? The four of them are working together to get Rock. That's the reason Waters has been riding Chip and the Rock. I've been suspicious of that connection ever since I saw the four of them all buddy-buddy down there at Sorelli's."

Soapy jumped to his feet. "That settles it!" he said. "I'm gonna see Zimmerman! Right now! Come on you guys!"

Petey's information substantiated Chip's worst fears. This was serious. Maybe he ought to reconsider that election idea of his. Not all blue laws were silly.

"Wait a minute, guys," Chip said softly. "This is my problem right now. At least until after I see Mr. Zimmerman on Tuesday. You've got to promise to let me work this out my way—"

"But what about the game tomorrow, Chip?" Biggie asked.

"We don't have a pitcher! Remember?" Soapy chimed in.

"Yeah," Speed added, "and there'll be a million people out there to see us play Stratford."

"I know," Chip said patiently. "I know how important it is, but I'm the one who's up to my neck in this mess—and I'd rather handle it my own way."

"Sure, Chip," Schwartz agreed, "but we want to win the game. It's your turn to pitch!"

"I want to win, too, Red," Chip said evenly, "but there's more to this than a game of baseball. Tell you what I'll do. I'll make a bargain. If you guys will keep out of it, I'll get into politics."

Soapy was first to catch on. "You mean you'll run for mayor?" he demanded excitedly.

Chip nodded. "That's right!" he said firmly. "I'm a candidate for mayor!"

CHAPTER 5

An Unfamiliar Seat

THE PACING began again, across the length of the comfortable living room to the windows facing out on the street. There was a short pause while black eyes under a furrowed brow peered out at the lengthening shadows of the late afternoon sun, then back to the fireplace and another pause while worried eyes studied the clock, the pictures, and the small vase of flowers on the mantel.

"Hank," Louise Rockwell said softly, "why don't you call Carl Zimmerman and have a talk with him? You need to put your mind to rest. You've worried all day."

The lines of Henry Rockwell's face relaxed and his eyes softened as he paused in his nervous pacing to look at his wife. Louise Rockwell was slender, delicate in appearance, with brownish-red hair graying at the temples, soft brown eyes, a turned-up nose, and a fair complexion. It would come as a surprise to anyone to learn she and Henry Rockwell had been married for nearly forty years.

Rockwell sighed. "I guess I'd better, Louise," he said uncertainly. "I can't get the rank injustice of the whole thing out of my mind. Besides, I don't know what in the world we're going to do for a pitcher tomorrow if Zim won't let Chip play."

He hugged her. "I'm sorry I spoiled your day, Louise," he said softly, "but we're right at the turning point of our season, and every game is important. Steeltown and Salem are playing great, and we can't afford to lose more than one or two more games. I don't approve of brawling, but what Zimmerman doesn't know is that Chip got into trouble defending me! If you're sure you don't mind, I think I'll go over to Zim's and have a talk with him."

Carl Zimmerman had been principal at Valley Falls High School for seven years. The first six of those seven years had been pleasant. However, Mark Condon had been elected mayor of the town the previous year, and he constantly interfered with Zimmerman's administration of the high school.

The incident at the game the previous day had been on the principal's mind ever since, and he knew that come Tuesday morning, if not sooner, Mayor Condon and some of his friends on the school board would demand a full explanation.

So it was understandable that Zimmerman was reserved when Henry Rockwell visited him late Sunday afternoon and pleaded for Chip's reinstatement. Zimmerman was patient but resisted persuasion. Yes, he realized Chip was important to the team's success and there was no other pitcher available.

Yes, he understood Henry Rockwell's predicament. But it was impossible for him to reinstate young Hilton without a thorough investigation of the incident.

AN UNFAMILIAR SEAT

After her husband had turned the corner and disappeared from sight, Louise Rockwell had opened the Sunday issue of the *Times* to the sports page. It didn't take her long to discover the article that had disturbed her husband earlier that morning.

Delford Scalps Big Reds, 10-0
by Muddy Waters

Hilton Suspended

Valley Falls's state champs were rudely surprised at Ohlsen Field yesterday when Delford lavishly applied a coat of whitewash to the red-faced locals. The visitors put on a three-ring circus for the near-capacity crowd of fans. They scored three runs in the opening frame and then pulled off a nifty triple play in their first time in the field.

The locals never got over that first inning, and Delford coasted to an easy victory. The expected battle of southpaws never developed. Bill Sheffer, star Delford left-hander, handcuffed the Big Reds and came near to adding a no-hitter to the day but slipped with two out in the fourth when Cohen touched him for a double. But that was as far as it went. Sheffer set Badger down on four pitches, and that lone hit was all the Big Reds could get.

Hilton Attacks Fan

In the fifth inning, just after Delford took the field, William "Chip" Hilton invaded the stands to attack a fan who had been good-humoredly razzing the home forces. The sudden, unprovoked assault shocked every person in the park and a near-riot ensued when Hilton's teammates joined him in the unwarranted attack. Combined efforts of indignant spectators and police officer Bob Gilbert soon broke up the melee, and the players returned to the field.

Principal Zimmerman showed resolute courage when he overruled Coach Henry Rockwell in ordering hotheaded Hilton from the field and suspended him from school. No information concerning possible assault charges against the youth was available.

Louise Rockwell's eyes were snapping as she turned the page to Waters's gossip column. She always read the spiteful writer's column—not because she was one of his fans but because she worried about his constant attacks on her husband. The very first words warned her of what was coming.

Times and Sports
by Muddy Waters

If Coach Rockwell had the ability to develop team fight on the field instead of in the stands, there might be a slim chance for the Big Reds to successfully defend their section and state laurels. As it is . . . .

It was just as well that the sound of footsteps on the front porch prevented Louise Rockwell from reading the rest of the vicious article. She hastily folded the paper and was placing it on the coffee table just as Henry Rockwell entered the room. One look at her husband's grim face told her that the trek had been in vain; Zimmerman had not relented.

Most coaches spend more time working out their team and campaign plans at home than they do on the field and in their offices, and their spouses usually join them in this extracurricular homework. Mrs. Rockwell was no exception. She knew every teenager who played for her husband, knew his strengths and weaknesses as well as her husband did. But she knew her husband best of all. They'd spent so much time together in such complete harmony that words were often unnecessary to express opinions or even thoughts.

Rockwell's tense face relaxed for a second, and his forced smile told Louise Rockwell everything. During all the years the two had shared their lives, they'd come to know and understand all the little gestures and actions that expressed the other's innermost emotions better than a thousand words. It wasn't strange then that no further reference was made to the controversy over Hilton's reinstatement.

So what should've been a day of rest from the worries of a hot baseball campaign turned out to be a frustrating, tiresome day, all the more difficult for Henry Rockwell to bear because of the inactivity. Later that evening he called Chip.

"You won't be able to play tomorrow, Chip. I talked to Mr. Zimmerman this afternoon, and it looks as though there's nothing we can do about it until Tuesday. I'll call you at home Tuesday morning. And, Chipper, I just want you to know I'm with you, and I appreciate what prompted you to do what you did. Everything will come out OK."

"Thanks, Coach." The boy's voice sounded calm and quiet, but Rockwell knew there was turmoil in the teenager's heart.

Mary Hilton, a supervisor at the phone company, was busy in her office Monday morning, but she just couldn't focus. Finally, she reached for the phone and tapped the numbers for John Schroeder at the Sugar Bowl.

"Chip is awfully upset, John, and I'm concerned about his suspension."

John Schroeder's familiar voice was reassuring. "Now, Mary, there's nothing to get upset about! I saw the whole thing! I don't know exactly what started the trouble, but I know Chip, and I know he had good cause for whatever action he took."

"John, the paper said it was assault."

Schroeder's voice was calm, but there was a decided edge to the tone of his words when he interrupted. "Mary, an unscrupulous, unreliable would-be sportswriter wrote that. You'd be foolish to pay attention to anything he writes.

"Petey and Chip are going to the game with Doc Jones and me. You just forget about the whole thing. I'll call Zimmerman the first thing in the morning."

That afternoon, Chip and Petey sat between John Schroeder and Doc Jones high up in the grandstand. It was the first time since he'd played for Valley Falls that Chip had ever sat in the grandstand and watched the Big Reds play baseball. In his junior year he'd been forced to sit in the stands during part of the football season because of a leg injury sustained in a car accident. Then, during the following months, he'd served as manager of the basketball team. But this was the first time during four years of baseball that he'd not been in uniform.

Chip felt strange sitting up there with the spectators. His eyes scanned the rows of townspeople who made up the typical baseball crowd. Directly below, he saw Jerry Davis and Richard Cantwell sitting with their heads close together, talking earnestly. Something alerted Chip, and he followed their glances toward the bleachers where Adams, Weaver, and their usual crowd were sitting behind the home team's dugout. Instinctively, Chip felt they were talking about him, and he was right.

AN UNFAMILIAR SEAT

"I don't see him," Davis was whispering to Cantwell. "Don't think he's here."

Cantwell looked around guardedly. "Don't worry," he said in a low voice, "if he is, Buck and Peck will find him."

Meanwhile, behind the Valley Falls dugout, Buck Adams and Peck Weaver were busily scanning the field trying to locate target number two.

"He's not in uniform, that's sure," Weaver grumbled.

Adams turned to study the rapidly filling bleachers. "Maybe he's in the crowd," he said hopefully.

"Hope so. We've got him on the run, and we might as well keep him goin'."

A few seconds later, Weaver elbowed Adams and muttered excitedly, "I've found him. He's up in the grandstand—last row—right next to Jones and Schroeder. See him?"

Adams nodded. "You're right! Well, looks like we'll have to pay a little visit to the grandstand."

"Not this afternoon," Weaver cautioned. "Schroeder and Doc Jones are too popular, and we gotta be careful."

"We won't do nothin'," Adams protested, "nothin' 'cept razz the grandstander a little bit. What's the harm in that?"

CHAPTER 6

A Familiar Seat

SOAPY SMITH groaned with every warm-up pitch from
the mound, and his discontent was echoed by almost
every Big Reds supporter in the park. The fans didn't like
it and Soapy Smith didn't like it. Soapy's only baseball
desire was to catch for his friend, Chip Hilton, and the
fans had come to see the Big Reds' star keep Valley Falls
in the race for Section Two honors. But on Rockwell's
orders, Soapy had limbered up and then walked slowly
across the diamond, grumbling and worrying all the way
but still determined to do his best. The stands began to
buzz.

"Where's Hilton? It's his turn to pitch."

"What is this? More of Rockwell's strategy?"

"It's not Rockwell's fault. That guy Zimmerman suspended Hilton."

"Sure, it was in the paper."

"What's the matter with Trullo?"

"Trullo pitched Saturday."

"So what? He's a big, strong kid."

"You know Rockwell—won't pitch a kid unless he's had three to four days' rest."

"Yeah, but we can't afford to lose any more games. Salem and Steeltown are tough."

"Someone ought to tell that to Zimmerman."

Quite a few grandstand fans were glowering at Zimmerman now, and the remarks became more pointed. But Zimmerman seemed oblivious to everything except his conversation with Burrell Rogers, Valley Falls athletic director.

"I don't know what to do about him, Rogers," Zimmerman said anxiously. "He's such a good man, but he just doesn't seem to understand that the board is determined to retire him."

Rogers nodded, understanding. "I know, Zim. I've tried to talk to him, but he's got a one-track mind. Says he's going to coach as long as he lives."

"Well," Zimmerman said, "he'd better be looking around for another job then because Mayor Condon has his school board allies all lined up to end his career at Valley Falls."

"What about Ohlsen and Jim Stanton and Trish Thomas? Condon has to have a majority, doesn't he?"

"Sure, but he controls the deciding vote, ex officio."

"That's right! I hadn't thought of that!"

A sudden roar swung their attention back to the game. Soapy was already in trouble. The Stratford lead-off hitter had punched a wobbly Texas leaguer right over third and had taken second when Lefty Peters couldn't field the ball in time for a play.

That upset Soapy and he walked the next two batters. Like the Big Reds' Biggie Cohen, Stratford's first baseman was a lefty and batted in the cleanup spot. He was loose up there, and Soapy made the mistake of trying to throw one past him. The tall, lanky batter met the fastball right on the nose, pulling it over Biggie Cohen's head in a low liner that hit fifty feet beyond the bag and rolled all the way to the right field fence just inside the foul line.

Nick Trullo was after the ball with the crack of the bat but misjudged the rebound from the fence so three runs scored, the hitter holding up at third. Before the side was retired, the cleanup hitter scored also, and when the Big Reds came in for their hits they were behind 4-0. When the fifth inning finally arrived, Stratford was leading, 7-0. The visitors' pitcher had blanked everyone except Biggie Cohen.

Chip's thoughts were bitter as he squirmed in his seat high up in the grandstand. Losing this game would practically eliminate the Big Reds from defending their state championship. Right now Salem was leading Section Two, with Steeltown right on their heels. It was too bad they'd lost to Steeltown a little earlier in the season at Steeltown. It had been a great game, and Trullo had pitched well, but the loss was on the books. If Stratford won this game—and it now seemed a cinch that they would—it would mean three defeats and only six victories. There were still six tough games to come, so it didn't look good.

Chip could hear Adams and Weaver relentlessly riding Rockwell, and a surge of anger flooded his thoughts. If it hadn't been for those two, these last two home games might have been won.

Adams and Weaver again had been unsuccessful in getting a rise out of Rockwell, so they decided to pay Chip Hilton a visit in the grandstand. They brazenly climbed over the railing separating the first-base bleachers from the grandstand and shoved their way into the last row of seats. From their new location they began to bait Chip—not directly, but by obvious reference.

"Right where he belongs—in the grandstand!"

"Yeah, once a grandstander, always a grandstander!"

"Notice he always has himself well surrounded."

"Yeah, quite a fighter—when he has a gang with him."

Chip clenched his fists and tried to concentrate on the game, but it required all his self-control. Only the memory of the conversation he'd had with his mom helped him ignore their cheap shots. Several times Petey Jackson gripped Chip's arm in sympathetic understanding.

Doc Jones and John Schroeder were angry, too, but they retained their composure. Long years of experience had taught them that such matters always balanced themselves out, one way or another.

Stu Gardner was deeply interested in this grandstand byplay. He recognized Adams and Weaver for what they were and knew the whole background of their feud with Rockwell. The scout's sympathies were all with the veteran coach and Chip Hilton. Gardner was no longer concerned about Chip Hilton's emotional balance. He marveled at the kid's self-control and the stories he'd heard about the problems between the two South Siders and Chip Hilton.

Gardner critically studied Weaver, noting the mean eyes; strong shoulders; long arms; wide, meaty hands; and thick body. Stu Gardner shifted his eyes from Weaver to Chip Hilton, sitting in the grandstand, and shook his head in disbelief. It just didn't add up. How did that kid, six-two and probably weighing no more than 180, ever get the best of Weaver? Not once, but twice, according to the stories he'd heard.

PITCHERS' DUEL

Gardner knew the kid was fast and in good shape, but those assets were nothing compared to Weaver's forty-pound weight advantage and his street experience. Anyway, the kid sure had nerve! Going over on the South Side all alone and standing up to Peck Weaver! Most people would have taken one look at Weaver, pivoted, and headed for home—fast!

When the dreary game finally ended, Chip cast a mournful eye at the 10-1 trouncing recorded on the scoreboard and silently trailed his three friends out of the grandstand. He was still quiet when he clambered in beside Petey in the back seat of John Schroeder's car. He was glad Adams and Weaver hadn't tricked him into another mistake; he was glad he'd been able to keep his head. Petey had been right. The whole plot was clear to him now, and he wasn't going to be stupid enough to fall for their bait again. They really weren't interested in him; they were after Rockwell. Well, they had played him for a fool and he'd fallen for it the first time—but that would be the last. He now had a plan that might help make things better—if he could win the election . . . and stay in school.

The Sugar Bowl closed early that night, and Chip thankfully headed home to do some studying. Strangely enough, none of the Hilton A. C. members were around. Chip didn't give it much thought; he wanted to get home, hit the books, and prepare for the meeting with Principal Zimmerman the next day.

Chip would have been astonished if he'd seen the gathering in the kitchen at Soapy Smith's house that night. Petey Jackson was explaining an idea, and Biggie, Red, Taps, Speed, and Soapy were listening intently.

"Soapy and I have our part all set," Petey said proudly. "See, here are the coupons we made on Soapy's computer. All you guys gotta do is get 'em in the hands of the right people. Soapy, you got the list? Good. Now, look. I'll call out the names and you let me know which ones you'll take. Write 'em down! All set?"

Half an hour later Petey sighed. "Well, that's that," he said grimly. "There are 180 seniors. How much is 180 times $1.25?"

"Two hundred twenty-five dollars," Soapy totaled. "But it'll only cost you half that amount, personally, Petey. We're in this deal fifty-fifty, you know. That's a lot from my pay!"

"You mean if Chip wins the election it'll cost each of you $112.50?" Biggie asked. "But if Chip isn't elected, it won't cost you anything?"

"He'll win," Soapy said stoutly, "and we'll pay! Don't worry about that!"

"Yeah, and they gotta present their coupon the night of the election," Petey warned. "Remember, it's a victory celebration."

Speed laughed. "It'll be a madhouse," he said gleefully. "A regular madhouse!"

Schwartz was nearly hysterical. "Oh, man," he chortled, "wait until Schroeder sees that mob. Can you imagine 180 seniors trying to get into the Sugar Bowl all at once? Oh, man!"

While Chip's friends were working on the Independent Party platform, Jerry Davis was proceeding with his all-out campaign against Henry Rockwell. The result of Davis's effort was reflected in the phone call Principal Zimmerman received from Mayor Condon at precisely nine o'clock Tuesday morning.

Zimmerman's voice was tinny and the hand holding the phone shook. "Yes, sir, I realize it's a disciplinary matter, but two weeks seems a little—

"But, Mayor, that would take him right up to the last game of the season—

"I have it right here. Let's see . . . Well, the season ends with the Steeltown game on the nineteenth. How about a one-week suspension? That would make him eligible for the Dulane game next Saturday."

Zimmerman's lips were pressed tightly together as the mayor's harsh, precise words echoed loudly through the receiver. When Condon finished, the worried frown lines on Zimmerman's brow had relaxed slightly and some relief was apparent in his tone as he completed the conversation. "Yes, sir. That's right, sir. One week, ending Friday, May 4. Good-bye, Mayor."

Ten minutes later Henry Rockwell appeared in Zimmerman's office. Rockwell was fuming. He wanted Chip Hilton reinstated immediately.

"Those men started that fight, Zim. They used a student to get at me. You must realize that!"

"That may be, Hank," Zimmerman said quietly, "but don't forget there's a matter of discipline involved. Hilton went up into the stands, and every student at the game saw him. I can't bring him back and excuse him just like that. I've got to penalize him. We'll have to suspend him for at least a week. That's all there is to it."

Later, a disgruntled Rockwell called Chip. "Chip," he said, "I'm sorry. You've been suspended from baseball until Saturday, May 5. I know just how you feel; I know this is unfair, but just the same, I can't do anything about it. We'll have to grin and bear it and hope for the best. By the way, Chipper, you hustle over to Zimmerman's office and get back in school."

"Isn't there some way I can get back for Wednesday's game, Coach?"

"No. We'll have to do the best we can, Chip. You just

stick it out up there in the stands and give us all the moral support you can."

Wednesday afternoon, Chip was again in the grand-stands with John Schroeder and Doc Jones. And once again Buck Adams and Peck Weaver got on Rockwell, resumed their baiting and jeering. Rockwell ignored them completely. This was an important game, and he and the Big Reds went all out in their efforts to win.

Nick Trullo pitched well enough, but the hitters could-n't bunch their hits. When the last Big Red went down swinging in the bottom of the seventh, Valley Falls had lost its third game in a row and the fourth of the season.

Muddy Waters took full advantage of the opportunity the next day, and what he said wasn't nice. Soapy and Petey were leaning against the counter, pouring over the *Times*.

"Look at this!" Petey growled, jabbing a long, skinny forefinger into the page. "How about this guy!"

Times and Sports
by Muddy Waters

Good-bye state and section championships. Delford probably took care of that yesterday after-noon at Ohlsen Field. The 5-2 score indicates how far and how fast the Big Reds have slipped. Delford has a season overall record of three wins and eight losses, which gives you a pretty good idea of the Big Reds' vulnerability.

Chip Hilton's bleacher escapade now begins to assume serious proportions for the Big Reds. Hilton's presence in the lineup in the last three games might have kept Valley Falls in the race. Then again, it might not have made any difference.

PITCHERS' DUEL

Some athletes can handle success. Some can't.

Some athletes confine their fighting spirit to the play of the game. Some don't. One big ego can ruin a team.

Many fans are wondering what kind of alibi Coach Henry Rockwell will come up with this time.

Remember last year's state gridiron championship? What happened this year? Nine regulars returned.

Remember last year's state hoop championship? What happened this year? The varsity five returned intact.

Remember last year's state diamond championship? What's happening this year? All but one regular is in uniform. By the way, the Big Reds have scored just three runs in their last three games. Their opponents have tallied twenty-six.

Chip Hilton's suspension ends Friday. Rockwell will undoubtedly start the bleacher champion against Dulane.

Wouldn't it be smart to equip Hilton with a pair of earplugs? Or should Rockwell address the Dulane fans just before the game and ask them to refrain from cheering because it might upset his temperamental star?

Soapy crumpled the paper in his hands and began to tear it to pieces. "Why, that . . . that . . . that . . . ."

Whatever Soapy meant to say was never finished; for once he was at a loss for words. But words weren't important right then. Petey Jackson knew exactly what his assistant meant, and he was completely in sympathy with Soapy's final gesture: the youth scooped up the bits of torn paper and threw them deliberately across the counter and out on the floor.

A FAMILIAR SEAT

Chip, in the back of the store, had heard the outburst from the vicinity of the soda fountain and had watched Soapy's destructive fury in amusement. But the shower of paper on the floor that Chip was supposed to keep immaculate roused him into action.

"Hey, what's up?" he demanded. "What's the idea?"

Soapy glared at Chip for a second and then the words came: "Jerk! Bum! Dork! Moron! Fool! Jerk!" Soapy spluttered, futile fury written on his scarlet face, bringing out every freckle as if it were confetti.

Petey answered Chip's questioning glance. "Muddy Waters," he said with disgust. "He's riding you and Rock again."

Chip nodded. "Yes, I know. Well, I guess I had it coming." He turned toward Soapy and gestured toward the littered floor. "Hey, look at my floor."

Soapy cleaned it up, still muttering and growling. All that evening he bewildered his customers with his continued references to "the bum, the dork, the fool, the jerk."

CHAPTER 7

Major League Scout

STU GARDNER had been in Valley Falls only a short time, but he'd learned a great deal about Coach Henry Rockwell. Through idle conversations, direct discussion, and personal observation, Gardner knew Rockwell was a solid citizen, a fine family man, a coach who loved his work, and a sincerely friendly person. Still, he felt slightly uncomfortable as he waited outside Rockwell's office. A few minutes later, however, all his awkwardness evaporated with Rockwell's warm greeting.

"Glad to know you, Stu," Rockwell said in a friendly voice. A welcoming smile played around his lips for a brief moment while his keen, black eyes studied the card Gardner had handed him. "With the Drakes? Good outfit! Sit down."

"Guess you know Del Bennett," Gardner began.

"Sure do! Known him for years! Great guy! Friend of yours?"

"Sure is, Coach, and that's why I asked him to write this letter. Mind reading it?"

MAJOR LEAGUE SCOUT

Rockwell took the letter and read it carefully.

State University
Del Bennett
Department of Athletics, Baseball Office

Dear Rock,   April 28

This note introduces Stu Gardner, an old friend and a former teammate of mine when I played ball and knew all the answers. I've found out since then that even Abner Doubleday didn't know them all. Anyway, I learned long ago that Stu Gardner is an honest person you can trust, and that's the reason for this letter.

Stu is interested in a couple of your kids (who isn't?) and wanted a letter of introduction. Give him all the breaks you can, but don't let him sign up that Hilton kid if there's any chance of him coming to school here.

Stu won't pull any fast ones, and I think it's great you two can get acquainted. Hope to see you up here for the championships.

                              Best regards,
                              Del

Rockwell folded the letter and placed it on his desk. "Del's a great guy," he said softly, a grin on his face, "but I didn't need the letter. I had you spotted a couple of weeks ago and expected some scouts to show up as soon as Hilton and Cohen and a couple of the other kids got ready to graduate. Well, what's on your mind?"

Gardner wasted no words. "You named them," he said simply, "Hilton and Cohen!"

Rockwell sighed. "Yes, they've got it. They're big league all right, but they're both planning to go to college. I'm pulling hard for them to do just that."

He spread his hands flat on the desk and leaned forward, his face suddenly serious, black eyes staring hard into Gardner's. "You'd agree with that, too, wouldn't you, Gardner?"

Gardner tilted his head sideways and nodded reluctantly. "Well, yes, Coach, I go for the college plan if a kid is a good student and wants the education." He breathed deeply, trying to hide the disappointment in his voice before continuing. "But sometimes a kid is better off taking advantage of his opportunities when they come. Especially if money is important to the family, as it appears to be in the case of these kids."

"You have something there, Gardner, but the parents of those boys, and the boys themselves, are looking forward to a college education. They're both good students, and they're ambitious. Don't forget, they'll be little more than kids when they finish college. They'll have lots of time left for professional baseball."

Rockwell studied Gardner closely. What he saw in the veteran scout's face must have pleased him, for the hard, set expression on his own face softened.

"Look here, Stu," he said kindly, "I know this is a big disappointment to you, and I know exactly how you must feel. Because I like you and respect the way you do business, I'm going to introduce you to those two kids right away. Naturally, I expect you to refrain from trying to get them to sign a contract or even to broach your desire to sign them until after graduation. OK? Then, if anything goes wrong with their college plans, you'll at least have an acquaintance with them and probably have the inside track. As I said before, college years fly by pretty fast, and they'll still be kids anyway when they get through. You'll have the contact and their confidence. OK?"

On Friday the *Yellow Jacket* announced the forma-tion of the Independent Party with Chip Hilton in the mayoral slot. The minute the paper went on sale, Soapy and his committee went to work. The unexpected politi-cal move created surprise and indignation in the ranks of the Home Rule Party and the Citizens Party, and they almost forgot their own campaigns in the excitement. Chip's teammates were enthusiastic, and once again Henry Rockwell's baseball team was filled with political fervor. However, Rockwell's mind was on Saturday's game with Dulane.

The Big Reds were surprised Saturday morning, May 5th, to see a suntanned stranger join Rockwell in the front seat of the bus when it pulled out for Dulane. There was some speculation about who he was, but Chip's reinstate-ment and the lift his return had given the team were too important to arouse very much curiosity in the appear-ance of a stranger. The Big Reds were intact again, and Soapy expressed their feelings when he said, "Salem and Steeltown may not know it, but their honeymoon is over!"

That afternoon Stu Gardner sat in the Valley Falls dugout throughout the game. He didn't talk to Rockwell or the players; he just sat there as quietly and as unob-trusively as possible.

Coming home that night the big bus rolled steadily along, the singing and the chatter keeping pace with the speeding wheels. The Big Reds were on the prowl again, and everyone was in step. Chip was tired but happy. He'd never felt better than that afternoon out on the hill. He had all his stuff, and for the first time in a long time, there'd been no razzing by Weaver and Adams from the stands. For a brief moment this thought worried him, but he quickly dismissed it. Why spoil a wonderful day thinking about guys like that? Hadn't he pitched a no-hitter that afternoon?

At exactly 9:30 the bus stopped in front of the Sugar Bowl. The happy ballplayers bounded out and were immediately mobbed by their loyal fans.

Rockwell stopped Chip and Biggie as they were leaving the bus and asked them to drop over to his house the next day to meet a friend. When they arrived the following afternoon at three o'clock, they weren't surprised to find the stranger who'd traveled with the team to Dulane sitting on the porch with the Rock.

"Chip, Biggie, Mr. Gardner is a scout for the Drakes, and he's been watching you two for a couple of weeks, since the draft is coming up next month. He hoped you'd be interested in being drafted and playing for them as soon as you graduated."

Gardner smiled ruefully. "That's right, men. I had hopes of signing you for our club, but Coach Rockwell has put the brakes on that. Said both of you are planning to go to college." He paused expectantly, but the two boys were nonplused. They looked uncertainly at each other, and it was Rockwell who broke the awkward silence.

"That's right, isn't it, Chip?"

Both boys nodded and then Rockwell continued. "I thought it would be a good chance for you to learn something about major league opportunities—contracts and bonuses and all that. Stu, suppose you tell us about the procedures your club follows in signing high schoolers to contracts."

Gardner took over then, and for the next hour explained legislation with respect to signing high school players, the bonus, and other rules. When he finished, Gardner asked the boys if they had any questions.

"I don't want to say no to a major league contract, but I want to go to college. Even so, I'm going to have a tough time getting good marks in college," Biggie said hesitatingly, "and I've been wondering if clubs ever sign players who want to try college first."

"Yes, that's been done. There's no rule against that. Of course, such a player would be ineligible for college baseball," Gardner explained. "You see, as soon as an athlete signs a contract, he becomes a professional. Quite a few players have been signed after they graduated from high school and have been paid a monthly salary while they were in college. But they couldn't play college baseball. Oh I suppose a few might have been signed up secretly and still played college ball, but it isn't honest and it isn't ethical. My club, the Drakes, will never get involved in such things. Nor will I."

Shortly afterward, Chip and Biggie thanked Rockwell and Gardner and headed for the Sugar Bowl. They'd learned a lot about major league organization and administration that afternoon, and each was excited by thoughts that someday he might have the opportunity to sign a contract, get a bonus, and do all the things he'd dreamed about. But first, there was college and an education.

Chip remembered something Rock had said. He could still hear Coach Rockwell's earnest voice: "An education is an asset that lasts a lifetime; no one can ever take it away! Money and friends may vanish, but an education sticks forever!"

CHAPTER 8

Stingaroo! Stingarii! Stingaree!

EARLY MONDAY morning Rockwell received a call from Principal Zimmerman's office. "Now what?" Rockwell muttered as he made his way along the broad hall to the school's main office. A call so early in the morning was unusual, and Rockwell had a hunch it meant more trouble. Zimmerman's first words proved him right.

"I've got some bad news for you, Hank."

Rockwell's brow furrowed deeply as he looked at Zimmerman. "You don't mean Hilton again?"

"Er . . . well, not entirely, Hank," Zimmerman said slowly. "Something more important. I hate to tell you this, Hank, but I think you ought to know Jerry Davis, Muddy Waters, and the rest of the crowd who have been after your job are . . . well . . . making progress."

Rockwell shook his head impatiently. "Don't let that worry you, Zim. They can't hurt me. The board of education has the last say on that issue, and I've known

J. P. Ohlsen and Jim Stanton and Trish Thomas for thirty years. They're my friends!"

"But how about old man Davis and Frank Greer and Dick Cantwell?"

"Well, they're not my friends, Zim, but they have no reason to dislike me—none I know of, at any rate."

Zimmerman shrugged. "Maybe not, Hank, but don't forget Davis is Jerry's father, and Greer and Cantwell side with him in everything."

"Sure, but they only make up half the board, and it takes a majority to vote on issues and decisions."

"Yes, Hank, but I happen to know a lot of pressure is being put on Mayor Condon, and he's ex officio chairman of the board."

"I'll never quit," Rockwell said thinly.

"You'll have to quit sometime, Hank, and you've had a great career. Your pension will amount to nearly as much as your salary. What have you got to lose?"

"Money isn't everything," Rockwell said grimly. "No, Zim, I just happen to like my job—and the kids."

"But you're past the usual retirement age, Hank, and besides, you've been here thirty-eight years."

"Thirty-seven," Rockwell growled.

"Well, thirty-seven then, Rock, but a teacher who reaches the age of sixty-three can retire. Besides, a teacher who has served thirty-five years in this public school system can also retire. You qualify on both counts."

"Qualify! Hah! What about a person's ability to do a good job? I don't think there is another person, young or old, who knows more about my job or will do a better job than I can do with all my years of experience. Do you think some youngster will know more about kids than I know?"

"No, Rock, I don't believe that at all. But I don't have the say in this matter, and I just wanted to let you know what you're up against. Davis is very determined."

Rockwell grunted. "They're up against something too. They won't force me out if I can help it." He shrugged his shoulders impatiently. "What would I do? I'd go crazy!"

There was a long silence as each was busy with his own thoughts. Rockwell finally broke the silence.

"You said something about Chip."

"Oh, yes, but it's not very important."

"Anything that concerns Chip Hilton is important, Zim. You know that!"

"It's not about baseball, Hank. It's about the student political campaign. He's the Independent Party's candidate for mayor, and, well, in view of his recent difficulties, I'm afraid I can't permit it."

"But Zim, that's not fair! What's the baseball incident got to do with the senior political campaign. That kid's been penalized enough! He was out of baseball for three games! Anyway, he's a student in good standing!"

"It is fair, Hank. The boy was reinstated in baseball, and that's enough." Zimmerman's voice was firm and a bit testy as he continued. "The administration of student activities is solely in my hands, Hank, and that's my decision."

Rockwell could not shake Zimmerman's determined stand. He left the office thoroughly disgusted with Zimmerman and his excessive ideas concerning discipline. There were a number of unusual situations and changes developing at Valley Falls High School that the coach didn't like and couldn't understand. Zim acted almost as though he were afraid for his job or something.

Zimmerman could have cleared up all of Rockwell's uncertainty if he'd told him about the mayor's call he'd received at home that morning. Condon had insisted Zimmerman disband the newly formed Independent Party at once.

"I won't have this splendid student activity turned into a farce," the mayor had fumed. "That party must be disbanded immediately and Hilton withdrawn from the campaign!"

Zimmerman caved in, but resentment against the mayor's continued interference was building with each passing day. His position was becoming unendurable.

Zimmerman resolved that his next principalship would be in a town where the government leaders dedicated themselves to serving the people. Mayor Condon seemed more interested in persecuting a high school kid who'd incurred his friends' anger and was running in an election against his own son. Zimmerman shook his head and grunted, "Condon is probably afraid Chip could win."

Rockwell's bitter mood remained sour and carried over into practice that afternoon. It was reflected in the crisp tones of his voice and in his impatient directions.

Chip didn't know what was wrong with the coach, but he knew what had dampened his own spirits. Zimmerman had tried to soften the blow about the election, but the decision had been hard to take. Chip had walked out of the principal's office and back to his homeroom badly discouraged. He'd said nothing at the time to his friends, nor did he say anything that afternoon when Zimmerman called a special assembly and announced that the Independent Party was being withdrawn from the campaign.

Soapy, Biggie, Speed, and Red, however, didn't take it without comment. They were outraged, as were others. Some faculty members—surprised by the principal's announcement—even discussed the democratic process in their classes.

The sudden blow had floored Soapy, and his only recourse was a strong verbal condemnation of Zimmerman. "Why, that jerk," he exploded, "that jerk!" That was the extent of Soapy's reaction to the announcement at the time, but his agile mind was busy through practice that afternoon.

The futility of the whole situation affected the Big Reds' practice session that afternoon too. Rockwell was smart enough to realize the workout was wasted effort. After brief hitting practice and an even shorter fielding drill, he sent the team twice around the field and then to the showers.

That night the Sugar Bowl was quiet and deserted. None of the ballplayers were around. Instead, they were holding a strategic planning session at Soapy Smith's house. With the exception of Chip, every member of the Hilton A. C. was there, as well as every member of the team. As usual, Soapy was doing most of the talking.

"Look," he said, "I got an idea!"

"Treat it gently," Biggie said dryly. "It's all alone in a strange place!"

Soapy sent a withering look in Biggie's direction. "No wisecracks," he commanded. "This is serious! Dead serious! Look, we're gonna beat that Zimmerman at his own game! We're gonna elect Chip, anyway—"

"But Zimmerman threw the Independents out," Red interrupted.

"So what! Now look, we gotta move! We've got to call every senior in town. Zimmerman can't stop us from voting the way we want to! That's why they have the little booths, so we can vote the way we want!

"Our constitution and our whole government's been built on voting the way we feel and believe." Soapy beamed self-consciously, then continued proudly, "Why, my last paper for Mrs. Mitchell was about democratic voting procedure, and she told me it was the best paper she got all term. I got an *A!*"

Everyone groaned, but Soapy merely lifted his eyebrows in disdain. "Well," he demanded, "don't you believe it?"

Schwartz chuckled. "Well, maybe," he drawled. "But what about Republican voting procedure?" he asked, grinning broadly and winking at everyone.

"They're democratic too," Soapy said seriously. "Now, listen . . . hey . . . that wasn't funny, Red. This is important stuff."

While Chip's friends listened, Soapy unfolded his plan to outwit Zimmerman and assure the election of Chip Hilton. Meanwhile in other homes, other Valley Falls residents were also talking about the forced withdrawal of Chip Hilton from the campaign. A few of the kids running were gloating—exultant because of the unexpected ouster of a dangerous candidate. But there were many students who didn't like it, and they were wondering if there wasn't something they could do about it.

Among those who gloated because of Chip's elimination from the election were Jerry Davis, Muddy Waters, and several of their allies, particularly Buck Adams and Peck Weaver.

"I wish we could fix that kid once and for all!" Weaver said with venom.

"Maybe we can," Adams said thoughtfully. "I've been thinkin' maybe we could push him into another fight and then get Davis to put some pressure on the mayor to get Hilton thrown out of school. Then Pretty Boy would be outta baseball and outta school."

"You think Condon could make Zimmerman do that?"

Adams laughed contemptuously. "You kiddin'? Condon's got that guy. Zimmerman's scared to death of the mayor! Sure he'd do it!"

"Well then, what are we waitin' for?"

"Nothin' much, except we don't want to make any mistakes. We gotta be careful. The kid's popular, and we don't want to have any problems with the law right now."

"I got it!" Weaver said suddenly. "Look, we'll tell Gilbert—he's the only cop they ever send to the games— we'll tell him Hilton has been threatenin' us. Tell him the kid said he was gonna get us with his boys. Then we'll get Hilton steamed up at one of the games. Let's see . . . the Steeltown game's scheduled here for the sixteenth. That's it! We'll do it on the sixteenth! We'll set up Hilton and then, when he reacts, we'll have Gilbert as our proof. Get it?"

Adams slapped Weaver on the back. "Hey," he said with exaggerated surprise in his voice, "you're gettin' smart! That's just the ticket! We'll tell Gilbert about Hilton and ask him to watch our backs when we go to the games."

"Yeah . . . but what if he hears us razzin' Hilton?"

"So what? Everyone razzes ballplayers. What we want to do is get Hilton mad enough to make him climb up in the stands again. See what I mean? Then Davis can have Condon step in and make Zimmerman throw Hilton outta school. Rockwell will be up against it for pitchers again, and the town'll get on him, and we'll be rid of both of those guys for good."

Tuesday's classes at Valley Falls High School were lively, to say the least. Principal Zimmerman and the faculty expected the day before the senior election to be exciting; they'd gone through the experience before and thought they were prepared for anything. But they'd never seen excitement like this on election eve. In homeroom, in the cafeteria, and in every class, one topic and only one topic interested the students: the election. The enthusiasm carried into the classrooms because most of the teachers' lessons focused on some aspect of the election process.

Coach Henry Rockwell believed a noisy locker room filled with happy baseball chatter was an indication of good team spirit and was the trademark of a championship team. So that afternoon as he dressed in his office, there was a satisfied smile on his face as he listened to the excited voices and loud laughter in the Big Reds' dressing room below. The smile faded a few minutes later, however, when he descended the steps to the locker room and listened to the conversation.

"Can't miss! Bet they don't get ten votes!"

"Gotta get at least ten; there's twelve of 'em running."

"OK, then twelve!"

"Hey, Soapy! What you gonna do for money next month?"

The clackety-clack, clack-clack of Rockwell's spikes on the iron staircase usually subdued the clamor, but not this afternoon. He wasn't even noticed. Striding past Pop Brown without a side glance and without his usual, "Hello, Pop," Rockwell slammed out the door. The veteran trainer looked after him fearfully. "Someone's gonna catch it," he muttered. "Gonna catch it good! Wonder what's wrong with him?"

Chip was dressing quietly in front of his locker. He'd tried all day to be cheerful and conceal the hurt in his heart. He'd tried to laugh with the others and join in the election excitement, but it just didn't work. He finally gave up and concentrated on the next day's game with Parkton. Still, he just couldn't figure out why Biggie, Soapy, Speed, and Red were so enthusiastic about the elections.

Out on the field a little later, Rockwell tried to figure it out too. He knew his team was up to something, but it wasn't baseball. For a second his temper flared, but a second thought brought him back to the realization that these boys were concerned right then with something more important to them than practice, Henry Rockwell, and the game with Parkton.

"It's the election," he whispered to himself, "sure as anything! They're up to something, and it concerns Chip!"

Rockwell noticed that Chip took no part in the discussions, and that gave him an inkling to the mystery. "Of course," he whispered again, "that's it! I knew they wouldn't let Chip down. Well, whatever it is, I hope it's good—and it works."

That night, Chip was further bewildered by the political enthusiasm of the Hilton A. C. and by the activity that centered around the Sugar Bowl.

Cars filled with students passed in front of the shop all evening with the passengers shouting, "Stingaroo! Stingarii! Stingaree!"

Speed's Mustang, parked in front of the big Sugar Bowl window, was decorated with big question marks. All evening, Big Red seniors came into the Sugar Bowl and whispered mysteriously with Soapy Smith and Petey Jackson.

Chip kept pretty busy in the storeroom that evening, but like John Schroeder, he was mystified by the constant parade. Both would have been completely bewildered if they could have heard the conversations.

"Hey, you're not a senior, beat it! Campaign material is only for seniors!"

"Soapy, what's this coupon for?"

"Here's the Chip Hilton Victory Menu! Look, you get a choice of the Hilton Victory Meal One—burger, fries, and a medium drink—or the Hilton Victory Meal Two—pizza, onion rings, and a medium drink—or the Hilton Victory Meal Three—ice cream sundae or a banana split. Now, remember our campaign slogan: Stingaroo, Stingarii, Stingaree!"

Wednesday morning was unusually quiet for an election day. Except for "Stingaroo, Stingarii, Stingaree," which appeared on every chalkboard and was whispered when most seniors passed, the lack of election spirit was absolutely uncanny. That afternoon, classes ended early for the voting.

Principal Zimmerman followed the seniors along the main hall to Ohlsen Gymnasium. Zimmerman knew the students of Valley Falls High School, especially the seniors. But as he stood at the door of Ohlsen gym viewing the procession of voters filing in and out of the voting booths in the center of the basketball court, he sensed something was out of place; it was too quiet. And what in the heck was this "Stingaroo, Stingarii, Stingaree" business?

Zimmerman was right about something being out of place, and he might have been able to figure out that something if he could've seen the headline the editors of the *Yellow Jacket* were planning for the front page of that afternoon's special election issue.

The Big Reds' locker room was electric as the boys dressed for the game against Parkton. Runners kept dashing in with mysterious messages—then and all during the Parkton game. Chip sensed something was up, but he was too intent on his pitching to care. He only wanted to get out on the mound and keep Valley Falls in the running for Section Two honors. Still, he couldn't help feeling a bit disappointed that his teammates would consider anything more important than the game.

Rockwell had told both of his pitchers to warm up, but when the game began, Chip toed the rubber. The choice was right and Chip was right. He had the Parkton hitters handcuffed. Inning after inning passed, and the visiting batters were so helpless the Parkton cleanup hitter summed up their futility when he said, "He owns us!"

At the top of the seventh and final inning, when Chip flashed the first strike across the plate, the score was Valley Falls 7, Parkton 1. Five minutes later, there'd been no change when Soapy slipped the game ball in his hip pocket and dashed toward a startled Chip Hilton on the mound. But Soapy wasn't the only one dashing toward Valley Falls's star hurler—nor was he the only one shouting, "Hi ya, Mayor!"

CHAPTER 9

Political Games and Education

OUTSIDE, THE line extended around the corner; inside the Sugar Bowl, laughing seniors stood shoulder to shoulder. Inside or outside, it was a noisy crowd. Behind the counter, Soapy, Petey, Red, Speed, and Chip were swamped with orders and arguments.

"Give me a Hilton Victory Meal Number Three."

"Can you add strawberries and whipped cream too?"

"Hey, I didn't say mushrooms! I said pepperoni!"

"Where's my banana split?"

"Can I substitute fries for the onion rings?"

Red was worn to a frazzle. "How come you didn't get more help, Soapy? You knew Chip was gonna win, didn't ya?"

"You did say mushrooms!" Petey barked. "Anyway, we're out of pepperoni."

"Look, I gotta have your victory coupon! Soapy, did you get his coupon?" Speed questioned. "No? Well then, brother, you're outta luck! Bet you didn't even vote!"

PITCHERS' DUEL

Soapy and Petey's victory coupons came in that night—every one of them! Biggie, Speed, Soapy, Petey, Chip, and everybody else helped out serving the celebrating seniors. John Schroeder and Doc Jones were amazed as they elbowed their way through the crowd.

"What's this all about?" Schroeder demanded. "What in the world is going on? What are all these slips of paper for?"

Doc shook his head vigorously. "Beats me," he said, "I don't get it."

Soapy and Petey both tried to explain at once. "Er . . . well . . . Mr. Schroeder," Soapy began, "you see, Chip was elected mayor!"

Petey interrupted triumphantly. "And this is the victory celebration! Yeah—I mean yes, sir, and these slips of paper—well, they represent the Hilton victory."

"And you can take it out of our wages," Soapy announced.

John Schroeder was an understanding man, but right now it suited his purpose to pretend that he didn't comprehend. "I don't get this at all," he stated sternly, turning to look at Doc Jones. "Do you get it, Doc?"

Doc Jones shook his head again. "I still don't get it!"

Schroeder glanced around the milling crowd of high school seniors. "Looks like the senior prom! All right, you two, hustle back and wait on them. But as soon as they leave, you come back to my office! Skip the register, and put those papers you're collecting on my desk."

Schroeder and Jones managed to get through the mob and into the storeroom. There they began to laugh, and they were still laughing when Soapy and Petey appeared an hour later.

"Here you are, Mr. Schroeder," Soapy said worriedly. "And here's the special election issue of the *Yellow Jacket*. It explains everything."

POLITICAL GAMES AND EDUCATION

"Everything but the coupons we've been getting out front," Petey added. "Read the paper, Mr. Schroeder, first."

Schroeder took the paper, and Doc Jones inched his chair closer. Varied emotions were expressed on their faces as they read.

THE YELLOW JACKET
VALLEY FALLS HIGH SCHOOL
· May 9

Special Edition   *Vol. 31. No. 34*

Chip Hilton Elected Mayor

HILTON A. C. POLITICAL STRATEGY A SUCCESS
A Surprised Write-in Wins!

The Home Rule and Citizens parties were completely submerged this afternoon when the popular vote of the senior class shifted overwhelmingly to elect William "Chip" Hilton, the Big Reds' pitching star, to the office of mayor for the administration of the town's business on Friday, May 18.

Chip was the former candidate on the Independent ticket that Principal Zimmerman ruled ineligible last Monday. The write-in vote sets a precedent and moves Hilton and his write-in associates into control of the school's senior politics.

Hilton, himself, was completely in the dark about the events and was as puzzled by the slogan adopted, "Stingaroo, Stingarii, Stingaree," as were the Home Rule and Citizens parties.

A celebration is scheduled for tonight at the successful candidate's headquarters, the Sugar Bowl. This celebration will undoubtedly eclipse anything of its kind ever held in the history of Valley Falls High School politics. The democratic process has proven effective. See you at the Sugar Bowl!

Stingaroo! Stingarii! Stingaree!

Schroeder finished reading the story and turned back to Soapy and Petey. "What's this 'stingaroo' stuff?"

Petey gestured toward Soapy. "That was his idea, Mr. Schroeder. Soapy figured a little slogan would identify each one of Chip's supporters."

"What about all these slips of paper?" Doc Jones questioned.

"They're for the victory celebration. That is . . . er . . . Soapy and I used them to figure the total we'd owe for the food, drinks, and ice cream."

"That's why we printed all the coupons on my computer, Mr. Schroeder," Soapy interrupted, "so you wouldn't be out anything."

"I can understand that," Schroeder said softly, "but what if Chip hadn't been elected?"

"Well, then, sir, no victory, no celebration," Soapy explained. "The slips weren't any good if Chip wasn't elected. That's why we had so many seniors' support, and I guess one of the reasons we won."

Doc Jones coughed. "You mean the seniors sold their votes to you for a coupon, don't you?" he asked blandly.

"No sir, not at all! We gave a coupon to every senior who wanted one and never told anyone who to vote for," Soapy quickly declared.

Petey began, "Most of the school felt Chip got a bad deal when he was suspended from the team. Then when Zimmerman declared the Independents ineligible, even more students sided with Chip. Only he didn't know it!

POLITICAL GAMES AND EDUCATION

When one senior supporting Chip met another senior, he'd say 'stingaroo,' and if the other senior said 'stingarii', the first one would come back with 'stingaree'! It kinda spread like wildfire."

Soapy looked proudly at Schroeder. "That was my idea! Clever, wasn't it?" he asked.

John Schroeder and Doc Jones eyed each other steadily for a long second. Then they turned back toward Soapy and nodded soberly.

"Yes, that was extremely clever," they chorused.

Petey was worried. "I hope you can understand, Mr. Schroeder," he said anxiously. "Soapy and I meant to tell you all about it, but everything happened so fast, we didn't have a chance. The whole amount comes to $225."

"And that's divided by two, Mr. Schroeder," Soapy explained carefully. "You see, Petey and I went 50-50 on the proposition!"

John Schroeder nodded gravely and told the worried employees he understood the math calculations perfectly, and he expected an accurate accounting of each coupon. He solemnly warned the two that he didn't expect the Sugar Bowl to be involved in any future political campaigns and then sent them back to their work. After the two dejected campaign workers filed out, John Schroeder remarked, "There go two very loyal friends. Also sounds like the senior class voted with more intelligence than we adults did in the last election."

A smiling Doc Jones replied, "I think Condon and Zimmerman are in for a few interesting moments—and they deserve every second of it!"

Soapy and Petey were strangely subdued the rest of that evening, but the other members of the Hilton A. C. were too happy and too busy to notice.

Chip still didn't understand it all, but he'd learned enough about the event to know that he'd probably end up in front of Mr. Zimmerman's desk again. He was absolutely correct. At that very moment, the principal of Valley Falls High School was thinking about the election and Chip Hilton.

While supervising the voting tally, Zimmerman had discovered what the Big Red seniors had been up to and he was thoroughly enraged. William "Chip" Hilton, who led all the candidates with his write-in candidacy to a landslide victory, was most prominent in Zimmerman's thoughts.

The Big Reds' baseball captain had received practically every vote. Zimmerman was also disturbed that the editors of the *Yellow Jacket* had printed the story without his approval. He promised himself he'd use drastic measures to curtail the activities of all concerned.

The next morning Chip felt as if he were sitting on a powder keg, but nothing happened. Right after lunch, however, Principal Zimmerman called a senior class assembly and sternly announced the election was invalid and the results could not be accepted. A little later he called Chip to his office.

Chip stated he knew nothing about the election and, despite the principal's insistence, refused to divulge who'd been responsible for the voting. Finally, in desperation, the exasperated school head told Chip to go home and report back to his office the next morning at nine o'clock.

As soon as Hilton left his office, Zimmerman sent for the *Yellow Jacket's* faculty advisor and student editor. The session was a stormy one. Natalie Parker was an able student editor and stood her ground with considerable resolve.

POLITICAL GAMES AND EDUCATION

She'd reported that the principal had presided over the election, and that it had been a fair one. The results represented the wishes of the seniors. Additionally, she confided that the general student body felt Chip Hilton was being treated unjustly by the administration. Before the interview was over, everyone was talking at once and nothing had been resolved.

Baseball practice that afternoon was a farce. Chip didn't report, and Rockwell knew nothing about his suspension. Once Chet Stewart told him what had happened, the harassed coach appreciated the indifferent attitude of the Big Reds toward the workout.

"That's all!" he barked. "Take three laps and hit the showers!"

Rockwell spun on his heel and hurried toward the gym, stamping his feet, swinging his arms, and muttering every step of the way. Through the locker room, up the steel steps, past his office, and down the hall, the angry coach stormed, unaware of the damage his spikes were inflicting on the highly polished floor. But Zimmerman's office was closed. Rockwell shook the door furiously, muttered something about "banker's hours," swung around, and stamped back down the hall.

Down at the Sugar Bowl that night, it almost seemed as if the place were going out of business. It was so quiet that the few customers who did drift in spoke in low tones. Chip was buried in his books in the storeroom while Petey and Soapy whispered excitedly, their heads close together at one end of the fountain. A little later they were joined by Speed, Biggie, Red, and every baseball regular. Right after the Sugar Bowl closed, Petey and the Big Red ballplayers, minus Chip Hilton, met at a prearranged rendezvous and then headed resolutely for the Zimmerman residence.

PITCHERS' DUEL

Soapy boldly led the way up the steps and punched the doorbell. Zimmerman was sitting in the same chair he'd occupied during the bitter four-hour discussion with Henry Rockwell earlier that evening. Although he'd tried to justify his decision, he knew his position was weak simply because he'd let Mayor Condon influence his thinking and interfere with the administration of his job.

The indignant coach had told him some things he didn't have the courage to admit to himself. Rockwell's parting words had hit home, and he was still thinking about them. "Political games and education don't mix, Zimmerman," the veteran coach had said coolly just before he slammed the door.

Now, when the doorbell rang again, Zimmerman sighed in annoyance and started for the door. When he saw his visitors, he knew instantly the purpose of their call and reluctantly escorted them to the living room. An embarrassed silence followed the entrance of the boys. But a few minutes later, Petey began to tell the amazed educator all the details of the conversation he'd overheard between Davis, Waters, Adams, and Weaver at Sorelli's.

Then Soapy chimed in. "We'd have told you the whole story ten days ago," he said, "if Chip hadn't stopped us. Chip knew about it all along, but he said he'd handle it himself. We'd have let him do it, too, except for the election. Mr. Zimmerman, that election was on the level. The senior class elected Chip mayor, and they don't understand the action you took this afternoon in calling it illegal and expelling Chip. If the election was illegal, then every senior who voted for Chip should be expelled from school. You should expel all of us!"

Although weak, Principal Zimmerman was basically a good man. As he listened, his thoughts were racing.

POLITICAL GAMES AND EDUCATION

From the beginning, he had, as Rockwell had said, failed to stand for what he knew was right and educationally sound. One compromise had led to another, one appeasement to another. If he'd only told Mayor Condon no at the very beginning, instead of allowing him to get his foot in the school door, things would be very different. Zimmerman smiled to himself as he thought about the coach. Rockwell would've stepped on that foot instead of opening the door. His own weakness in buckling under to Condon had cost him the respect of his school. His action toward Hilton had cost him his own self-respect.

But it wasn't too late to take a stand. As Petey and Soapy talked, the administrator studied the intense faces of what might well have been considered Valley Falls High School's inner athletic circle. What he saw in those earnest faces pleased him, and it must have done something to him too. He surprised his listeners, and himself, by abruptly rising, extending his hand to each in turn, and assuring them that the information they'd brought threw a different light on the whole episode. He assured them he'd take it from here.

A puzzled throng of whispering, wondering students quickly filled the auditorium the next afternoon at two o'clock. Rumor had it that the staff of the *Yellow Jacket* would resign; Chip Hilton would announce his resignation from the office to which he'd been elected; and another senior election would take place that very afternoon. No one was prepared for the principal's initial statement—least of all, Chip Hilton.

After everyone was seated, Principal Zimmerman asked Chip to come forward. Chip, expecting further humiliation, made it to the platform some way, walking stiff-legged and feeling more self-conscious than he'd ever felt in his life. As he passed Natalie Parker's seat on the aisle, she whispered, "Hang in there, Chip."

At the top of the short flight of steps, Zimmerman surprised Chip by shaking his hand and leading him to the center of the stage. Waiting for the whispering and foot scraping to cease, the school head, looking calm and confident for the first time in days, smiled and startled everyone by saying, "Members of the faculty and students of Valley Falls, I want to introduce the senior who will serve as the mayor of Valley Falls on Friday, May 18th."

There was a stunned silence for what seemed a full minute before the principal's words registered, and then the room burst into a roar of applause. Chip found his way to his seat in a daze. He never heard Zimmerman say that the entire *Yellow Jacket* staff had proven themselves true crusaders in the field of journalism.

The other candidates, who'd smugly entered the assembly, sat quietly in their seats. The rest of the students were on their feet, cheering. As if guided by an irresistible force, the whole gathering started moving—moving for the doors, spilling out of the exits and out of the building. What a great ending to the school day for the seniors of Valley Falls High School!

CHAPTER 10

Pouring It On

NICK TRULLO was in trouble. His arm had been aching ever since he'd pivoted in the third and used Rockwell's pickoff play to catch a Dane runner off second base. The throw had been perfect; Speed Morris and Cody Collins had played it right; and the runner had been out by a mile. But the twinge in Trullo's arm had changed to an ache in the fourth, and in the fifth the pain in his deltoid muscle was continuous and intense. Trullo finished it out, but he sat quietly in the dugout holding his upper left arm tightly with his big right hand through the top of the sixth.

When he walked out to the mound in the bottom of the frame to take his eight warm-up throws, his arm felt as though it were a dead weight.

Rockwell had been trying every strategy and substitution he could think of to overcome the Dane lead, but here it was the bottom of the sixth and the run Dane had scored in the third loomed bigger and bigger. To make it worse, the Big Reds' bats had been silenced completely by Dane's strikeout king, "Bullet" Nichols.

Rockwell had kept Chip on the bench hoping to rest him up for Steeltown and planning to use his star hurler as a pinch hitter if a break came. But the Big Reds couldn't get to first base. This was a "must" game. Valley Falls had to win this one or else forget about the state tournament. In fact, all three games with Dane, Steeltown, and Salem were must games.

Chip had been cheering on every pitch and every play. Now he sent a barrage of encouraging words in Nick's direction. As he did, he noticed there was something wrong with Trullo's delivery. Before he could bring it to Rockwell's attention, the Dane hitters had pounced on Nick's nothing ball, and runners were perched on first and second with none away.

"Coach," Chip cried, "Trullo's arm's gone! Watch his delivery!"

But Rockwell was already on his way. "Time!" he called. "Time!"

Nick Trullo was no quitter. Every throw he'd made in the last two frames had been followed by a blast of fire that began just below his elbow and raced up his arm and through his shoulder. But he hadn't said a word; he'd tried to conceal the pain. The big southpaw wanted to win this one on his own so Chip would be ready for the big game with Steeltown four days away. Then he could take his turn against Salem three days after that, and they might be able to come through. But now, as Rockwell came striding toward him, Nick knew he'd gone as far as he could; he had nothing left.

Rockwell needed only one glance at Trullo's tense face to realize his player was in pain. The harried coach glanced out in right field toward Soapy Smith, pondered a second as he caught Chip's eye in the dugout, and then beckoned for Soapy. Then, placing an arm around Trullo's shoulders, Rockwell gently led a grimacing Nick Trullo off the field.

Chip was on his feet and out of the dugout just as Rockwell signaled Soapy. Before Trullo and the coach had taken five steps, he was beside them. Chip grasped Trullo's hand and looked into his eyes with empathy. "You did a great job, Nick," he said sympathetically. "Don't worry about it!"

"Coach, I can get 'em out for Nick." Chip turned toward the mound, waved Soapy back to right field, and motioned for Carl Carey to throw him the ball.

"Atta boy, Chip!"

"C'mon Chip! Humm-babe!"

"Mow 'em down, Chipper!"

But Chip didn't mow them down. He shook Carl Carey off until he got the right sign and then placed four pitches just out of the hitter's reach to fill the bases. Then he took a deep breath. Now the play was at any base.

It was good baseball, and it paid off. The hitter, too anxious, went after a fast one around his knees and pulled a bounder right at Chris Badger. Chris fielded it flawlessly, stepped on third, and nearly tore Carl Carey's glove off with his peg to home. Now there were two away and runners on first and second.

Chip had been sizing up the Dane hitters all through the game and had tabbed the batter facing him as timid. He liked to sidearm a righty and give him a tight pitch when the batter didn't like them close. This hitter didn't like them close and was soon called out with his bat on his shoulder.

Rockwell met the team in front of the dugout as they came trotting in. "Now, let's go get a couple of runs," he urged. "Come on! Last licks! Got to be!"

It didn't look good, and, in his heart, Chip knew it. Still, he pepped it up with the rest of them. Lefty Peters, up at the plate, was hitting less than two bucks, and Carl Carey, on deck, was almost as bad. Nonetheless, a guy sticks with his teammates; good or bad, Chip had to make them feel that they could do it.

He kept chirping away as he hefted two bats and mentally timed his swing with Bullet Nichols's heater. The big righty had lost none of his speed, and every pitch seemed to have a hop on it. But Chip wasn't worried; he liked to hit fastballs.

Lefty Peters wasn't any bigger than a minute as he stood up there, determined to follow Rockwell's orders.

"Make him pitch, Lefty. Make him pitch!"

"Get on, Lefty. We'll bring you in!"

Nichols smoked them in, but Lefty didn't give an inch. He just stood there, crowding the plate. He worked the count to two and one.

"Brush him back, Bullet! Brush him back!"

"Stay up there, Lefty! Look 'em over!"

"Get on, Lefty! Chip'll bring you in! You get on!"

Lefty dug in and crowded the plate, and that aggravated Nichols. He wasn't the kind of pitcher a hitter toyed with; he didn't like batters who took a toehold. A fast one streaked in, but it was too close and too fast, and it caught Lefty smack in his ribs. The ball thudded in with a vicious thump, and Lefty dropped. But there was a grim smile on his lips as he clambered to his feet, brushed off his teammates' hands, and trotted down to first. Lefty was on!

Chip moved into the on-deck circle, knelt down, and watched Nichols intently as he pitched to Carl. It was this inning and no other inning. Now or never. The whole season depended upon scoring at least one run, and it was going to be up to him no matter what happened to Lefty and Carl. Chip looked at the right field fence and then mentally kicked himself in the pants. Babe Ruth could point to a fence and deliver—but he was no Babe Ruth. He'd concentrate on meeting the ball.

Carey took a called strike, turned up his nose at a low and outside pitch, and then sent Lefty scampering to second on a fast-rolling bunt down the first baseline that the first baseman handled too late to make a play at second and barely in time to beat Carl to the bag. So there, in answer to the Big Reds' frantic pleas, was the duck on the pond. It was up to Chip Hilton to get it home.

Chip took his time getting around to the first-base side of the batter's box, tugging his batting helmet, pulling at his belt, wiping first the right hand and then the left hand across the front of his shirt, tapping his left shoe with the bat and then the right; but at last he was there and he dug in, got himself a good toehold. One brief glance sufficed to place the positions of the Dane outfielders. They had shifted far toward the right.

Bullet Nichols knew Chip Hilton, and so did the fans. Every Dane fan there remembered one or more football, basketball, or baseball games that the tall, slender athlete at the plate had broken up, and they decided to give him the works. They didn't think he could do it, yet they couldn't tell about this kid. Anyway, they'd give him all they had; maybe it would help. They rose to their feet with a roar of derision and taunts. Nichols did his part too. Hilton was a power hitter, and ballplayers who hit the long ball don't like to get all set and then be kept waiting. So Nichols fiddled around, smoothed out a little pile of dirt behind the mound, looked and faked at Lefty on second, and fiddled and fooled until the umpire behind the plate got nervous and barked, "Play ball!"

PITCHERS' DUEL

Chip stood in the batter's box, completely relaxed, bat resting on the plate. Then, when Nichols toed the rubber, Chip stepped back out of the box. The umpire glared at Chip and raised his hands. "Now what's the matter with you?" he growled. "Come on, play ball."

Chip laughed and waited until Nichols stepped back off the mound. Then he went through his batting ritual again and stepped up to the plate. Nichols didn't fiddle now. He took his stretch and threw a duster that came in like a streak of lightning, and he laughed delightedly when Chip avoided the speeding ball only by dropping flat on his face. Chip got up slowly, picked up his helmet, looked questioningly at the umpire as he dusted himself off, and then stepped back in the box.

Nichols came in then with an overhand slider that broke across Chip's belt and evened the count at one and one. He followed that with a change-up curve that fooled Chip for the one-and-two call, and Nichols was out in front. Nichols fired his fast one inside then, and it evened up the count once more. Right then, Chip decided he'd go for the next one; he wouldn't wait for the full count.

The big righty's slider was Chip's ticket. Although Chip's swing was late, there was a sharp crack and the ball took off in a screaming line over the shortstop's head, past the left fielder, and clear to the fence. Lefty was away with the hit and scored as Chip drove toward second. Then, the Dane left fielder made a mistake; he threw to the keystone sack. Chip couldn't believe it, but he took advantage of the miscue, turning on the speed and heading for third. It was close, but he beat the relay by an eyelash, sliding safely under the throw from the second sacker.

Chip got up slowly then and took his first real deep breath. A quick glance at the scoreboard reassured him;

POURING IT ON

it was all tied up! The Big Reds were back in the ball game! He glanced at Chet Stewart in the first-base coaching box and then at Collins. The little second baseman was receiving last-minute instructions from Rockwell and tapping his bat aggressively on the red clay. A second later he was at the plate, and Chip got the sign from Stewart. The squeeze was on, but Cody had to pick his own pitch. That put Chip on the spot, too, because the Dane infield was in tight, determined to cut him off at the plate.

Cody brought the crowd to its feet as he dumped a perfect roller down the first baseline and chased it so closely he had to swerve out of the base path to avoid the rushing first baseman. Chip slid in under the throw to put the Big Reds ahead by a score of 2-1, and Cody was safe at first.

Chip was up on his feet before the umpire roared, "Safe!" only to be knocked down again by his charging teammates who mobbed him all the way to the dugout.

Cody Collins, taking a short lead from first, was the victim of an easy Dane double play. Speed's hard line drive was snagged by the surprised first baseman who stepped on the bag and ended the Valley Falls threat. The Big Reds hustled out on the field for the bottom of the seventh with a one-run lead. Chip was still a bit breathless and took his time getting out to the mound. But the 2-1 score looked big now. Speed Morris helped out by stabbing a grass cutter far to his right and making the long throw to catch the runner by a step for the first out. The second hitter banged a vicious line drive right back to Chip who couldn't get out of the way and didn't even know how he caught the speeding ball. It brought a big cheer from the stands, and two were away.

PITCHERS' DUEL

That brought the game down to that famous "last out." It was the Dane center fielder and cleanup hitter. Every Dane fan was on his feet yelling for Pete to hit it out of the park. He nearly did it too. He caught Chip's fastball flush on the nose but pulled it foul. That gave Chip a scare and warned him that Pete liked the hard one. So Chip's change-up came twirling in for the second strike, and he was out in front. Then Chip fired a blazing fast one high outside, but Pete watched it go by without moving his bat.

Standing there, ball hand and arm dangling behind him, Chip thought of something: *Why not try the blooper?* He'd used it only once all year.

He shook Carey off until Carl finally remembered and smiled behind his mask. Chip nodded, wound up, gripped the ball with his fingernails, and pulled the string. The ball shot up and out and, after what seemed an hour, floated lazily down toward the plate, big as a balloon. Pete watched the ball coming straight down in the strike zone and then swung so mightily that he twisted clear around and fell to the ground. He was still sitting there looking for the hole in his bat after Carl Carey had tucked that third-strike ball in his pocket and headed for the Valley Falls dugout.

Mary Hilton had intently scanned her son's face the night before and had caught the fatigue in his troubled gray eyes. That was the reason she was moving around so quietly and keeping a protesting, meowing Hoops downstairs away from Chip's room this Sunday morning. It was 9:30 when Chip, dressed for church, finally appeared in the kitchen and kissed his mom.

"Sorry, Mom," he grinned sheepishly. "I crashed. I just couldn't get up."

POURING IT ON

"I know, Chip," Mrs. Hilton said softly, smoothing back her son's unruly blond hair. "You look a lot better this morning. Feel better, too, don't you?"

Chip's answer was to give Mary Hilton what they called his "carousel whirl." He lifted his mom high in the air and swung her around until they were both laughing.

"Whoa, Chip! You had too much sleep! Put me down."

After breakfast Chip plunged into the sports pages of the Sunday papers. Although Pete Williams lauded Chip's hitting and relief pitching, Muddy Waters took a different position.

Times and Sports
by Muddy Waters

Valley Falls won a game yesterday afternoon, defeating Dane High School and the great Bullet Nichols by a score of 2-1. But, the Big Reds lost Nick Trullo, because of overwork, and one more mark can be chalked up against the bleacher slugger Chip Hilton.

Trullo was forced to carry the whole load during Hilton's suspension, and the overwork strained his arm. Coach Henry Rockwell kept Trullo in the game inning after inning when anyone could see that the big southpaw was pitching solely with his heart.

Rockwell was undoubtedly saving Hilton for Steeltown. Is the Steeltown game that important? Important enough to risk ruining a kid's arm? Why does Rockwell persist in protecting Hilton at the expense of the other members of the team?

Chalk up yesterday's win to stellar fielding by the Big Reds and to little Lefty Peters's cleverness in working Bullet Nichols for a pass that led to the tying run.

Cody Collins was the real star, thanks to his clutch squeeze bunt that scored Hilton with the winning run.

Steeltown is in as far as Section Two is concerned. The Iron Men now have a record of 10 and 3 with two to go: the Big Reds here next Wednesday, May 16, and Southern at Steeltown on Saturday, May 19. The Iron Men should win both games without much trouble, from where we sit.

Valley Falls now has a record of 9 and 4. The Big Reds and the Sailors both have two to go. They meet head on at Salem, May 19.

A tightness constricted Chip's chest when he finished reading. Sighing deeply, he shook his head. What was Waters trying to do?

Minutes later he leafed through the rest of the *Times.* There were the usual world news features, which he read quickly, and then his eyes ranged over the page and came to a sudden stop at Muddy Waters's gossip column.

"No!" he muttered. "What's this—"

Muddled High School Politics
Traditional Senior Election Is Farce
Cheapened by Vote Rigging
by Muddy Waters

The annual senior election to determine the student administrators of Valley Falls on Friday, May 18, was held last Wednesday. For the first time in the history of this traditional activity, the election was a farce.

This reporter learned from reliable sources that the majority of the voters supporting the write-in candidates sold out for cheap refreshment promises payable at John Schroeder's Sugar Bowl.

POURING IT ON

That the school authorities will countenance this travesty of an important civic activity is inconceivable; that the young men and women who will graduate from our high school in less than two weeks would regard their responsibilities so lightly is incomprehensible.

In former years, the seriousness and sincerity accompanying the election made this extracurricular activity one of the most important events on the senior calendar. A number of Valley Falls's civic leaders have expressed their deep concern, and drastic action can be expected in the next few days.

William "Chip" Hilton, who was suspended from school two weeks ago for attacking a spectator at one of the baseball games, was the successful write-in candidate. It is difficult to believe that such strong-arm methods will be tolerated and rewarded, regardless of the importance of the group to the school's athletic program.

Chip was dismayed. "Well, what do you think of that?" he said aloud. "Why, that—"

"What did you say, Chip?" his mother called from the kitchen.

"Nothing, Mom," Chip answered, folding the paper hastily. "Just talking to myself."

Just about that time, in a small house perched high on the hill on the South Side, Buck Adams and Peck Weaver were gloating over Muddy Waters's columns.

"That Waters really pours it on," Weaver chuckled.

"Yeah," Adams agreed. "And now everything's set. Trullo's out and that means all we hafta do is get Hilton. Then we'll have Rockwell where we want him."

"We better work fast," Weaver warned. "They've only got two more games, and Hilton's good! He could beat

Steeltown and Salem both, all by himself! That would give 'em a record of 11 and 4, put 'em in the play-offs for the state!"

"Yeah," Adams agreed. "Let's see. Steeltown's 10 and 3 now. If Hilton beats 'em Wednesday, that would tie the two of them up. Who the Steelers play next?"

"Southern at Southern," Weaver breathed, "and those Tarheels are tough!"

Adams nodded his head decisively. "Yep," he said, "you're right! We gotta move fast! We'll get Hilton Wednesday afternoon!"

CHAPTER 11

Zimmerman Rulz

SOAPY SMITH was reading the age-yellowed pages of a copy of Valley Falls's city ordinances from 1850. "Hey, listen to this, guys! It says here, 'Every resident of Valley Falls must stand still when the clock strikes three o'clock to com . . . com . . . commensurate the construction of the dam above the city.'"

"It's *commemorate*," Biggie growled.

"OK, OK, commemorate," Soapy retorted defiantly, glaring at Biggie. "What's the difference? Commensurate, commemorate, compensate—it's all about commerce, and that means money!"

Red rolled his eyes and exclaimed, "Get the thesaurus quick! Our king of malapropisms is at it again!"

Upstairs in the family room over Chip's lab in the basement, Mary Hilton glanced at her watch and smiled. This Sunday afternoon meeting of the Hilton A. C. was evidently important. The boys had been in noisy session nearly two hours.

It was important all right, important to Chip's plans for the following Friday. He made sure his friends understood how serious he was.

"Come on, guys," he said firmly. "We're wasting time. Let Soapy finish! We've got lots to do between now and Friday. Go ahead, Soapy."

"OK," Soapy said in an aggrieved tone. "I'm ready. Hey, here's a good one. 'Peanuts must be eaten in the store in which they are purchased. Furthermore, it is illegal to stand more than five minutes in any one place.'

"'Lollipops may not be sold between the hours of 8:00 A.M. and 5:00 P.M.'"

Soapy chuckled. "Oh, man, this one will do in old man Thomas. It says here 'A man may not wear a beard unless he pays a fee or a tax.'

"Here's a great one! 'It's against the law in Valley Falls to sell beer unless the establishment also has a kettle of soup brewing.' I guess you could say Mike Sorelli's in the soup! Hah!"

Soapy let out a hoot of laughter. "Oh, boy! Listen to this! 'No person in Valley Falls may give his sweetheart a box of candy weighing less than five pounds.' Wait'll the boss gets a load of that!"

A few minutes later, Soapy finished reading the list of laws his department had selected to enforce on May 18. Then Chip took over.

"Now here's the list of offices. Write them down. Biggie, you'll serve as chief of police, and judging from the number of laws you'll have to enforce, you're going to need some special officers. It's up to you to select a good force from the other grades. You're going to be busy!

"Nick, you'll be the sheriff, and you'll need some help. And Cody, you're Nick's assistant. Speed, you'll take

Judge Graham's place since your dad's a lawyer; Chris will be city engineer.

"Soapy, you'll be chief of detectives and it's up to you to choose your own staff. Red, you'll be the fire chief.

"Carl, you'll be auditor. Here's a list of the other officers."

"What about these girls?" Carl Carey asked doubtfully, looking at the list of names. "You mean we have to put up with them?"

Soapy snorted with glee. "Look who's complainin'," he said boisterously. "The great Romeo's protestin'! Not!"

"Some of the girls have key roles," Chip said patiently. "Mr. Zimmerman and I made the selections. Natalie Parker is council president."

"Hey," Soapy said brightly, "who's the deputy mayor, or is that question too personal?"

"Er . . . no," Chip said hesitantly. "Mr. Zimmerman appointed Caitlin Gibson—"

"Caitlin Gibson!"

"The cover girl?"

"Miss Valley Falls?"

"Take a letter, Chip, dear!"

"Yoo-hoo! Yoo-hoo, Mayor!"

Chip finally got them quieted. "Well, I guess that's it," he said, reddening.

The principal of Valley Falls High School expected a call from Mayor Condon first thing Monday morning, and he wasn't disappointed. The call came exactly at 9:05 A.M., and Zimmerman's voice was precise and steady when he answered.

"Yes, Mr. Condon. Fine! . . . Oh, the election. Yes, that's all settled. . . .The paper was right, Mayor; Hilton was elected. . . .Why, yes, Mr. Condon, he was elected fairly, practically by a unanimous vote. . . . But write-in voting is legal, Mayor. . . . I'm sorry, sir, but I won't do that! . . . No, William Hilton was elected, and the matter is closed. In fact, all the offices are filled and can't be changed. I'm sorry you feel that way, Mayor, but there's nothing I can do. Good-bye, sir!"

Zimmerman's face was set in grim lines when he hung up the phone and leaned back in his chair. Well, that was that! He'd better get busy on that new job search! He had a hunch Valley Falls would be a memory, come September.

Around the horn and back to Cohen—that's the way the Big Reds hustled the ball around the infield. That's also the way they zipped it around when they took the field Wednesday afternoon. Biggie always handled the ball last before it went to the pitcher. Now, as he palmed and twisted the ball, trying to remove some of its shiny newness, he walked close to Chip.

"This is a big one, Chipper; bear down all the way. They're good, and they beat us before, remember?"

Chip remembered. The Iron Men had beaten Trullo 3-2 earlier in the season to give the Big Reds their first setback. He hadn't forgotten that, and he wasn't going to forget this was a must win. If Valley Falls lost today, they'd be completely out of the race, and Steeltown could be sure of the runner-up spot, maybe even the championship. Yes, this was a *must* win. And it was all up to him. Today and Saturday too. Nick would be out for at least two weeks, maybe for the play-off games at State. If . . .

The Valley Falls-Steeltown sports rivalry was as keen as constant pressure could make it. Year after year the two high schools were among the leaders in the state and usually figured in the stretch race for Section Two honors. This year Steeltown had one of its best teams in years, and their earlier win over the Big Reds at Steeltown had given them confidence, making them cocky. The Valley Falls fans noticed the visitors' arrogance immediately, and when the Big Reds trotted out to start the game, the state champs were surprised by the intensity of the crowd's support.

Behind Chip, his teammates were pepping it up, confident of his ability to take Steeltown. It was great to play on a team with that kind of spirit, and Chip swallowed hard to get rid of the choked feeling in his throat. Then he toed the rubber, took Soapy's sign, and everything was forgotten except the batter at the plate.

"Just you and me, Chipper," Soapy bellowed. "Give it to me, baby! Just you and me! Fire it in!"

Chip felt relaxed and right. His fast one had a hop on it, and his change-up curve was finding the corners. He got the big end of the Steelers' batting order one, two, three.

But Bob Lennox was just as good, equaling Chip's performance. Lennox was a master of the soft stuff, tantalizing curves and the slow, twisting knuckler. Today his control was perfect.

That's the way it went for three innings, each pitcher matching the other. Both hurlers were pitching perfect ball. Neither had been touched for as much as a single. Chip kept the pace in the top of the fourth, holding the Iron Men helpless. With the last out, he was greeted by a roar of approval from the stands. As he walked across the limed first baseline, he lifted a hand to touch the bill of his cap in response to the applause. Then he saw Adams and Weaver. They were sitting right behind the Big Reds' dugout, eyes mean and angry, glaring straight at him. Something warned Chip that they were up to something; they'd been too quiet. . . .

PITCHERS' DUEL

Chip continued to the dugout without another glance at the stands. Then it happened! Each time the Big Reds had come in from the field, Adams had watched for an opportunity to pull the trick he and Weaver had planned. A quick glance around convinced him that this was the time. Two men seated beside Adams stood up and leaned over him briefly, concealing the heckler from view. Buck leaned forward, over the top of the dugout, and spat a full mouth of tobacco juice into Chip's face.

Chip had expected something, but Adams and Weaver had been so quiet he was completely surprised by the sudden action. Without thinking, he changed direction and charged around the dugout, heading for the stands and Buck Adams. Then, just as he placed his hands on the railing in front of the first row of seats, he stopped short.

What am I doing? They're leading me straight into another trap!

He stood there for a second, clamped his jaws to still the angry words rushing through his mind, and then turned away. He was still wiping the tobacco juice from his eyes when he ducked under the sheltering roof of the dugout.

The incident passed unnoticed by the spectators and Chip's teammates, but Rockwell had seen what had happened. He leaped out of the dugout, hoping to be in time to stop Chip from reaching his tormentors. But Chip was on his way back and never saw Rockwell. Both heard the derisive laughter of Adams and Weaver, and a burning flame of anger almost got the best of each of them.

Chip wasn't the only one finding it difficult to bring himself under control. Rockwell, too, had just about reached the end of the string with Adams and Weaver. Perhaps it was fortunate for everyone concerned that

Speed Morris stopped on the way to the bat rack at that moment for instructions.

"Should I wait him out, Coach?" Speed asked.

"Let's try it, Speed," Rockwell said certainly. "You've got a good eye; make him pitch to you."

Speed worked Lennox for the first walk of the game, and the hopeful roar of the home crowd drowned out the abuse Adams and Weaver continued hurling at Rockwell and Hilton.

The pass Speed had drawn was the first break for the Big Reds, and Rockwell was back to his old self, concentrating on the game. Red Schwartz followed the signs, and his sacrifice bunt put Speed on second with Biggie Cohen up at the plate. The big southpaw had a good eye, and he worked Lennox for the full count. Then Biggie smacked a slow curve in the hole between right and center for two bases, and Speed trotted across the plate with the first run of the game. Lennox really went to work then, setting Chris Badger down with two fastballs and a change-up curve in three fast pitches, and his soft stuff had Soapy Smith swinging from his heels and out with a pop-up to the catcher.

The excitement aroused by the short flare of action and the first score of the game gave Chip a chance to regain his composure. He was still jumpy, however, when he walked out to the hill for the top of the fifth. He tried to forget the incident by concentrating on Soapy's target and pouring his warm-up pitches through the strike zone, but it wasn't easy. The South Side contingent wasn't going to let him forget.

"What's the matter, loser? Can't you take it?"

"Yeah, your tough man act frightened us."

"Need help to get over the fence?"

"Boo, Hilton, boo!"

PITCHERS' DUEL

Steeltown didn't know what it was all about. The fans behind their dugout didn't get it either, but they were quick to pick it up. Soon, loyal Valley Falls cheering was drowned out by the shouts leveled at the Big Reds' star hurler.

Despite Chip's resolve, it was impossible to ignore the crowd. His fastball streaked in, but he was aiming too carefully at Soapy's target and his control faltered. He put too much on the ball, tried too hard, and the result was the loss of just a bit more of his control. The first two pitches barely missed the corners for the count of two and no, and the Iron Men's taunts came rolling out to the mound in an ever-increasing crescendo.

Baseball fans seem to sense the emotional instability of a pitcher, and these rabid rooters knew Chip Hilton; they knew when he was right and when he was upset, and they'd figured correctly now. The batter drew four straight balls for Chip's first walk of the game. In spite of Soapy's delaying tactics, Chip also walked the second hitter.

Rockwell called time then and walked slowly out to the mound. He was joined in the huddle by Soapy, Biggie, Speed, Cody, and Chris as the fans whooped it up. The mingled roar of support, gibes, and digs reverberated around the little group, drowning out all hopes of normal speaking, and Rockwell was almost shouting as he addressed Chip.

"Forget it, Chipper. Don't fall for the trick. You're too smart! Don't let them get your goat with a little bit of razzing."

Biggie threw a heavy arm around Chip's shoulders, gripping his friend's arm with a hamlike hand. "Come on, man," he cried, "remember what this game means. Push 'em in there. Let 'em hit! We're behind you."

Rockwell's black eyes locked intently on Chip's face, and when the teenager nodded and thumped the ball into his glove, the veteran coach knew the crisis had passed. Four long years of training and observation had endowed Rockwell with a complete understanding of Chip Hilton. He took the ball from the glove, tossed it to Biggie, and leaned close to Chip. "Walk the next hitter," he said loudly, "then go to work!"

The bases were loaded. Every fan in the park was on his feet, yelling at the top of his voice, and the taunts of the South Siders were lost in the din. Chip wouldn't have heard them anyway. Once again he was the hungry hurler from Valley Falls who rated number one in the state.

Chip eyed the batter, crowding the plate, obviously up there to wait him out. The base runners danced on the base paths, daring a throw, but Chip wasn't interested. He shook Soapy off until he got the sign for the fast one, inside, around the waist. He flashed two of them "in there" for a nothing-and-two count, which moved the batter back from the plate. Then he pulled the string on a change-up and the Iron Man was another K in the scorebook, missing the ball by a country mile.

The next hitter was tall and angular with power written all over him, from the high-held bat to the full-stride stance. Chip noted the away-from-body elbows and the steady bat. Here was a pull hitter, a clutch hitter. Maybe he'd go for a fast outside-corner pitch. The Iron Man went for it, reaching out with his bat instead of stepping into the ball, and Chip was ahead, nothing and one.

Soapy called for a change-up, but Chip's keen gray eyes had noted the short stance the batter had assumed. The hitter didn't seem comfortable up there, and Chip figured the slugger was guessing with him, looking for a curve. He waited for Soapy to call for the fast one and then sent the ball zipping right across the letters, in close. It was a perfect pitch for a pull hitter, but the batter wasn't ready and realized his mistake too late. His hasty forward stride dipped his bat, but he still got a piece of the hopping ball, sending a lazy liner to short right center. Schwartz raced in on a dead run, snared the ball from his shoelaces, and pegged a perfect strike to Soapy.

The runner on third had been fooled by the ball, figuring at first it would drop in front of Schwartz for a hit. He had started for home, only to reverse to tag up when the frantic third-base coach chased him and he saw his teammates waving him back.

When Schwartz caught the ball, the Iron Man lost his head completely, threw caution to the winds, and raced for home, determined to force a play at the plate. He didn't have a chance. Soapy charged gleefully up the base path and met the runner head-on, hand gripping the ball like a vise in the pocket of his glove. He was still holding the "precious pill" when he somersaulted to his feet and tossed it to the umpire.

Chip yelped thankfully at Soapy and high-fived Schwartz as the redhead came ambling into the dugout. He didn't know what he said and Red didn't either. But it didn't matter because the thundering roar from the stands drowned out his words and those of everyone else.

The Big Reds couldn't score in the bottom of that hectic inning, but it wasn't important. Chip held Steeltown scoreless all the rest of the way, and the Big Reds didn't need their bottom-of-the-seventh turn at bat.

Going home in Speed's newly repaired Mustang, Chip, pleasantly relaxed, was oblivious to the boisterous yells of Soapy and Red. He was replaying the game and thinking about the near run-in with Adams and Weaver. A smile creased his lips. He hadn't fallen into their trap this time, and he wasn't going to fall the next time. . . . Guess the win this afternoon had surprised everyone. Valley Falls and Steeltown were tied for second place now, each with identical records of 10 and 4.

Salem was sure of the championship. The Sailors had won fourteen and lost only one. Chip wasn't going to forget that game or the duel with Rick Parcels for a long time. Parcels was good! Anyway, the Big Reds had won that one just as they had won today and by the same score. Maybe he could beat Parcels again. It would be up to him, all right. Nick's arm was still bad.

Just suppose the Big Reds beat Salem, and Southern trimmed Steeltown. That would put Valley Falls in the play-offs! Anything could happen once a team got to the tournament. Valley Falls had come in second in Section Two once before and had gone to State and won the championship. Maybe they could do it again. It was a crazy thought, all right, but lots of crazy things happened in baseball. They'd be in a tough situation, though, if they won the runner-up spot. What would Rock do for another pitcher? Well, anyway, they had a chance. Wishful thinking maybe, but who could blame a guy for dreaming . . . for hoping . . . for trying?

CHAPTER 12

The Moral Edge

"HI YA, MAYOR! How's things down at City Hall?"

"Yeah, Mayor, when you gonna clean up the place?"

"Going to put a new sidewalk in front of your house?"

"When you goin' fishing, Mayor? How about a ride?"

Chip smiled and hurried back to the storeroom. All morning at school the big topic had been the important victory over Steeltown. But by lunchtime, the game was old news and tomorrow's administration of Valley Falls by the senior class held everyone's attention. During the rest of the day at school and at baseball practice, Chip had heard little else. Now, at the Sugar Bowl, he was busy in the storeroom with his plans. But he took time to read the story in the *Post*.

High School Seniors Take Over City Government
William Hilton Mayor-for-a-Day

Tomorrow is the day when the elected or appointed Valley Falls seniors fill city offices for a day. The students will report to their offices bright and early tomorrow morning to get acquainted with their duties. The complete list of officers follows:

Mayor:	William Hilton
Deputy-Mayor:	Caitlin Gibson
City Council:	Natalie Parker (President)
	Roberto Parente,
	Jennifer Cooper,
	Marcy Single, Aynsley West,
	John Kim Jr.
City Judge:	Robert Morris
City Engineer:	Christopher Badger
Sheriff:	Nicholas Trullo
Deputy:	Cody Collins
Chief of Police:	Benjamin Cohen
Chief of Detectives:	Robert Smith
Fire Chief:	Eric Schwartz
Auditor:	Carl Carey

Chip finished reading the paper and rechecked the names of his staff. For an anxious moment he wondered what the reaction would be to his carefully laid plans, but that feeling persisted only for a second. Chip knew he was right, and, as things stood, there wasn't much he could do about it now. He was committed to his course of action.

Chip and the city council seniors reported to the mayor's office the following morning at nine o'clock. Photographers from the *Post,* the *Times,* and the *Yellow Jacket* smiled cheerfully when they spoke to Chip and the council members, but they were quite serious about the pictures.

"Hold it, Mayor! Just a minute now!"

"That's it! Move a little to the left, Miss, er, Gibson."

"Chip, look right at the deputy-mayor. Oh, wow!"

Chip glared at Orndorff and resolved to discuss certain things with the *Yellow Jacket* columnist.

After the publicity shots, Mayor Condon escorted Chip and his staff to the town's executive offices and left them with a pleasant "Good morning and good luck!"

Chip walked gingerly around Condon's desk before sitting in the big leather chair. "This is something," he said slowly, softly rubbing his hands across the top of the polished mahogany.

"Push all those buttons and see what happens," Red Schwartz urged, pointing to the intercom. "Let's start something!"

"Never mind that," Chip said firmly. "We've already started something. First item on the agenda is a meeting of the council."

In the council room, Chip reviewed the day's plans and received a unanimous vote of confidence.

"That settles it," he said quietly. "We'll proceed according to plan, beginning at two o'clock this afternoon. Don't forget now," he warned, "the baseball team's got to be at practice at 3:30, and we've got to beat Salem tomorrow. That means all the alternates will move up to their jobs after the team leaves for practice." He turned to Caitlin Gibson. "You'll be acting mayor, Natalie, and it's up to you to follow through."

At twelve o'clock Mayor Condon appeared to escort Chip and the council members to the Chamber of Commerce luncheon at the Valley Falls Inn. It was the biggest turnout of the year. As he and his council members were led to places at the head table, once again his heart jumped as he scanned the smiling faces of the men and women, as well as his classmates, who were seated at the various tables. A lot of these luncheon guests were in for a big surprise before this day was over.

After the luncheon there were several brief speeches before Mayor Condon was introduced. He spoke glowingly about the seniors' enthusiasm and predicted great futures for "these fine young men and women." When Condon introduced "our new mayor," it took all of Chip's willpower to master his feelings, but he made it. As the representative of his classmates, he thanked Mayor Condon, the Chamber of Commerce, and the citizens of Valley Falls for their kindness and thoughtfulness in giving his class the opportunity to learn so much about city government.

Mayor Hilton found it extremely difficult to shorten the after-luncheon pleasantries and humorous references, but he tactfully explained he was plagued by serious city problems and some of them were dynamite.

"You never know when the fireworks are going to cut loose when you hold public office," he said cryptically.

Half an hour later, practically every senior was at City Hall. By two o'clock, the photocopied plans worked out by the mayor and his cabinet were distributed. Then the dynamite, to which Mayor Hilton had referred, exploded.

Two hours later the members of the Valley Falls baseball team trotted out on Ohlsen Field chuckling and laughing and imbued with more spirit than Rockwell had seen all year. He didn't waste time wondering about it; he simply chalked it up to the momentum of the Steeltown victory, hustled them through a fast workout, and sent them home for their suitcases.

"Bus leaves at six o'clock sharp," he admonished. "Be on time! I want to get to Salem by eleven o'clock! We'll eat at Weston. . . ."

PITCHERS' DUEL

The bus pulled out at six o'clock sharp, all right, followed by the strains of the Big Reds' marching band's victory salute.

"They must think we're off for the state tournament," Schwartz remarked.

Soapy snorted. "Give us time, pal," he chided. "This time next Tuesday we'll be on our way. Right, guys?"

The affirmative roar was music to Rockwell's ears. He sighed contentedly. This team was up! Way up! He leaned back in his seat, closed his eyes, and relaxed. He'd missed the seniors around school. It had been a slow, quiet day.

Henry Rockwell would've been surprised and amazed to hear that the past afternoon had been one of the most event-packed in the town's history and that some people were holding him responsible. At that very moment, in fact, Jerry Davis was sitting in Mayor Condon's office talking about the Big Reds' coach.

"Rockwell's behind this, Mayor. I'll bet he planned it!"

Condon nodded. "I wouldn't be surprised," he said bitterly. "He's always backed up that Hilton kid. I never heard of such a thing."

"Well, why don't you do something about it? Why don't you get the board to retire him? Right now! Ohlsen's out of town, and you'd have a majority."

Condon slowly shook his head. "No, Jerry," he said thoughtfully. "The timing's bad. Everyone would tie it in with the things that the kids turned up this afternoon, and there'd be more trouble."

"But why couldn't you hold a confidential meeting? Why not pass it through and then keep it quiet until the end of the school year?"

"Nope," Condon demurred. "Rockwell's popular and the team's doing well. If the kids won the state championship again this year, Rockwell would be the talk of the town. Might even beat me for mayor."

"But what if they lose?" Davis persisted. "It's a veteran team, and the fans in this town are hard losers. They'd blame Rockwell, wouldn't they? Wouldn't that be enough of an excuse along with his age and everything?"

Condon deliberated. "Probably would," he said slowly, "but what makes you think they'll lose?"

"Well, for one thing, Salem's the best team in the state. They'll probably win tomorrow, and that'll knock the kids out of the race—unless Steeltown loses too. Even if they do beat Salem and go to the state tournament, they haven't got a chance to win the championship. Nick Trullo's out with a bad arm, and Hilton's the only other pitcher."

"Hilton's good!"

"Sure he's good! But Rockwell won't use an iron mike unless it has had three days' rest! And to win the championship you have to play three games in four days. Who's going to pitch? Besides," Davis said menacingly, "I happen to know a couple of guys are out to get Hilton, but good. He'll be lucky if he gets to pitch one game!"

Condon's sharp eyes deeply probed Jerry Davis's pale blue eyes. Then he nodded decisively. "All right," he said shortly, "I'll do it! You get your father to submit the proposal and force it through. Understand?"

Davis laughed confidently. "Don't worry about that! The old man hates Rockwell nearly as much as I do, and he's got Cantwell and Greer under his thumb. It's a lock!"

John Schroeder and Doc Jones had dinner together that night at the Valley Falls Inn and spent nearly two hours laughing and talking about the day's events. The amusing aspects were enjoyed by hundreds of other citizens that evening, too, but many people failed to find anything humorous in the developments. Buck Adams and Peck Weaver were furious and blamed their predicament on Henry Rockwell and Chip Hilton.

"That kid thinks he pulled a fast one, doesn't he?" Weaver growled.

"Yeah," Adams muttered, "that's what he thinks. He'll pay for this! What goes around, comes around!"

Mike Sorelli was also fuming as his eyes flashed back through the long, narrow, empty room. Normally, every pool table in the place was busy by this time. Mike decided to see Mayor Condon the first thing in the morning. He'd spent a lot of time and money campaigning for that guy. He couldn't make money running a business unless he had customers, and Mike Sorelli couldn't compete with the free pool tables available in J. P. Ohlsen's recreation center unless he had certain inducements to offer.

Chip wanted to get a good sleep so he'd be in great shape for the game, but the strange bed, the long trip, and thinking about all the things that had happened that day led to a restless night. He was still tired when the Big Reds took hitting practice the next afternoon. A little later, warming up with Soapy, he saw Rick Parcels throwing in front of the home dugout. It was to be another pitching duel of right-handers. He shifted his eyes quickly to Nick Trullo lobbing the ball to Carl Carey. Nick's arm was a little better but not good enough. Chip would have to go all the way.

A tremendous cheer greeted Rick Parcels when he walked out to the mound to start the game. Parcels had lost only one game all year: a 1-0 shutout to Chip Hilton and the Big Reds. The home fans wanted to even that score. So did Rick Parcels. Chip knew this was going to be another last-out battle after Parcels's first pitch. Rick had all his stuff, and he retired the Big Reds in order.

Chip's fatigue vanished as soon as he toed the rubber; he was fast and his control was perfect. He matched Parcels' performance, but it required more throws. The Sailors were waiting him out, looking over every pitch, working him to the limit. It was good strategy. This was the fifth straight game he had worked, five games in fifteen days.

Going into the last of the sixth, Parcels had eight strikeouts and had held the Big Reds to two singles. Chip had set nine Sailors down on strikes and had yet to yield a hit.

The first hitter topped a slow roller toward Badger and streaked for first. Chris swooped in on the ball and fielded it perfectly with a bare-hand pickup. Then he fired the ball in a continuous underhand throw to first. The stocky infielder had made this throw all year, and not once had it gotten away; but this time the ball took off in a fast rising slant over Biggie Cohen's head and out to Carl Carey in the right-field corner. The runner lit out for second, made the turn, and gambled on Carl's arm. It was a good gamble, and he went into third standing up. Carey's throw was wide of the base.

The home fans jumped to their feet when the ball sailed over Biggie's head. This was the break of the game. All at once Chip felt tired; he had that let down feeling that grips an athlete in a tense moment of emotional stress. Then he gave up his first walk of the game, and that put runners on first and third, none away.

The runner on first scampered down to second on the very next pitch. Soapy didn't even try the throw. The Salem fans really had themselves a time when Chip's fastball sailed away from Soapy. Both runners scored before an agonized Soapy could retrieve the bounding sphere. Chip came to life then, striking that hitter out and getting the next two on pop-ups to Cohen and Badger.

When the visitors trotted in for the top of the seventh, every Big Red knew it was now or never. Then and there they got a shot in the arm. Several unimportant scores came over the loudspeakers, but the last one was the thriller.

"Southern 9, Steeltown 7!"

The Big Reds' cheer was spontaneous, but it died just as fast. Steeltown's loss meant a sure tie for the runner-up spot . . . but if they could win . . . if they could take the Sailors . . . they'd be in the play-offs!

Soapy was up, freckled face serious and determined. He slashed a worm burner through the box and over the keystone sack for the Big Reds' third hit of the game. Chip, in the circle, turned toward the dugout for instructions, but Rockwell waved him toward the plate, signaling that he was on his own.

Parcels hadn't forgotten that other game and the screaming liner his opponent had smashed into right center. Rick remembered too well how Chip Hilton had stretched that hit into a triple that led to the only and winning run of the game. He looked toward the dugout and called time.

Chip knew what the Sailors had decided in the brief huddle as soon as Parcels began throwing for the corners. Rick wasn't going to give him anything good, but neither was he going to put the tying run on first. So Chip waited them out, waited for the good one that never came. As he trotted down to first, he was still happy. The tying run was on now, and there was no one down. He swiftly calculated Cohen's position in the batting order. Cody, Speed, Red, and then Biggie. If they could only get another runner on, Biggie would do it. Biggie had to do it!

Rockwell showed his hand. He knew this was the big break and that a mistake now would probably mean the loss of the game. The Big Reds hadn't been able to hit their weight against Parcels in two games. So, he'd lay it down and keep laying it down until he could get Cohen up there to win the game.

Cody Collins was the Big Reds' lead-off hitter, and he could bunt with the best of them. Cody delivered, dropping a shallow one fifteen feet down the third baseline, the ball hopping back almost as soon as it hit. The Sailor third baseman, playing up, got the ball, pivoted for the throw to third, then changed his mind and threw to first. But Cody's short legs could move, and he beat the throw by a step. Chip, dancing off second, breathed a deep sigh of relief. Biggie would get his lick now, if someone on base didn't get caught.

Speed Morris had hit in the Big Reds' push along slot for three years, could place a bunt on a dime, and run like the wind. Without hesitation, Rockwell made the decision and the sign for the bunt came through. Speed justified Rock's confidence, squeezing Soapy home and advancing Chip to third and Cody to second. He nearly beat Parcels's throw to first. That brought in the first run of the game for the Big Reds with one away and Schwartz at bat. Red was a steady slugger and hit in the number three spot. He was good in the clutch.

Rockwell knew the Big Reds. Again the sign for the squeeze came through, and again the play worked. Chip was in like a streak of lightning, flashing across the plate with the tying run before a disgusted Rick Parcels could make the play at home. But his string-throw to first had

Red by twenty feet. So there they were, all tied up, with Cody and the winning run on third, two away, and Biggie Cohen at bat.

So far, the big southpaw had been able to reach Parcels safely only once in seven trips to the plate. But thirty seconds later he'd raised that average to .250. Collins had scored to put the Big Reds ahead 3-2, and Biggie was standing on second base. But that was the end of the "big break." Chris Badger went down swinging, and Biggie was stranded on second.

Chip's earlier tired feeling had disappeared when Cody stomped across the plate with the tie-breaking run. In fact, Chip felt as though he hadn't thrown a ball in a month when he dusted his fingers with the rosin bag after his warm-up. Then he turned on the heat and hopped his fastball past the hitters, setting the Sailors down in one-two-three order, putting the Big Reds in the state championship play-offs!

Main Street was dark and deserted when the bus pulled into Valley Falls that night. Two or three dim lights gave evidence that a few all-night restaurants were still open, and irrepressible Soapy organized a hamburger party. Chip, however, hurried home, anxious to tell his mom about the game.

Mary Hilton, who'd been reading in bed with a sleeping Hoops curled at her feet, slipped downstairs when she heard Chip open the door. She listened with warm eyes to his enthusiastic description of the game. When Chip finished, she thrust the papers into his hands.

"Read the stories, Chip," she said excitedly, "they're sensational. All I've heard since yesterday afternoon has been about the seniors and your administration. Everybody in town's talking about it."

THE MORAL EDGE

City Administrators' Faces Red
High School Seniors Responsible

Valley Falls will remember Friday, May 18, a long time! City officials experienced anxiety yesterday because of Senior Day, and developments continue. Directed by teenage mayor William "Chip" Hilton, the student administration created some real political ripples! The ground that covered his brief term testifies to his organizational ability.

After a short speech at the Chamber of Commerce luncheon, Mayor Hilton called a meeting of the city council to discuss several important issues, and the council approved several resolutions. The first resolution gives more autonomy to the school board, and the second enjoins all city administrators from personally interfering in school management.

Third, a surprise enforcement of many of the forgotten city ordinances was recommended, and a list was turned over to Sheriff Nicholas Trullo.

The final move responsible for most of the administration's embarrassment was the decision to swear in one hundred special police officers—male and female students—to process and serve a multitude of fines and warrants under the direction of Police Chief Benjamin Cohen and Chief of Detectives Robert Smith.

Here are some highlights of the students' actions:

1. Several raids on South Side illegal gambling establishments, operated by two well-known locals, were successful. Accompanying reporters and photographers substantiated the evidence. Cards, gambling slips, and other gaming material were confiscated.

2. The city auditor, Carl Carey, issued Mayor Condon's office a bill payable to the city treasury for the labor and materials used in making improvements to a personal residence by city workers.

3. The proprietor of a local poolroom was served with a warrant for permitting gambling and the consumption of alcohol on his business premises.

4. Sheriff Birks's office was issued a letter of reprimand for permitting the unauthorized use of city-owned vehicles. The department was further reminded that the use of city vehicles is limited to official business, and employee dependents are prohibited from operating city-owned vehicles.

5. Fire escapes on several buildings were condemned, and a number of building owners were advised that their smoke detectors and sprinkler systems were inadequate.

6. The one-day fire chief, Eric Schwartz, and other city officers tried to condemn Valley Falls High School as a fire hazard but were overruled by the council.

Valley Falls's citizens got a laugh out of the high-handed action of the teenage "city leaders," but there are many thoughtful adults who see beyond the youthful antics in the lively one-day administration.

This paper suspects that the students were giving their elders a lesson in government as well as in civic and moral responsibility. It is also suspected that some timely and sensible reforms may come about because of this enlightened government.

Chip was relieved. "Sounds pretty good, Mom," he said earnestly. "I was kinda worried."

Mary Hilton smiled brightly. "Never worry about doing the right thing, Chip," she said softly. "Now, off to bed."

The excitement and events of the past two days had exacted a heavy toll. Now that Chip's mind was at ease, he fell asleep almost as soon as his head touched the pillow. In the next room, Mary Hilton, happy to have her son safely home in bed, breathed a little prayer of thankfulness.

She was especially glad Chip hadn't seen the accusing article Muddy Waters had splashed on the front page of the *Times* that bitterly attacked the ill-advised denigration of an esteemed, democratic tradition by certain members of Henry Rockwell's baseball team.

CHAPTER 13

Blueprint for Revenge

EARLY MONDAY morning, five prominent Valley Falls citizens were sitting in the council room waiting for Mayor Condon. Jim Stanton and Trish Thomas were uneasy and wary. They weren't sure they wanted to remain active in the present school board administration. The fact that J. P. Ohlsen was out of town and that the special meeting had been called in spite of his absence also prompted their deep concern.

On the opposite side of the table, lined up side by side as usual, Jerry Davis Sr., Frank Greer, and Dick Cantwell were conferring in low voices. These three men worked hand-in-glove with Condon and didn't care who knew it. When the mayor entered a few minutes later, their amiable welcome contrasted sharply with Stanton and Thomas's reserved greeting.

Condon was in a bad mood and didn't even try to temper the viciousness of his immediate attack on Rockwell.

"This man has gone too far," he said angrily. "There isn't the slightest doubt in my mind that Rockwell was behind every despicable act perpetrated by those high school smart alecks last Friday. I happen to know the whole thing was planned by the senior members of the baseball team, and that in itself is an indictment of the moral stability of Rockwell's leadership.

"I've called this special meeting to determine just what action we should take to remedy the situation. Yes, Jerry?"

Jerry Davis Sr., proprietor of the area's largest jewelry store, was completely wrapped up in his oldest son. He'd come well prepared for the opening he now saw, and quickly followed Condon's lead.

"You're right, Mayor," he said firmly. "I, too, feel the time has come when we should do something about Rockwell's retirement. The man has outlasted his usefulness, and, if this meeting is in order, I move that Henry Rockwell be retired at the end of this current school year."

The grim lines around Condon's mouth relaxed into a smile while Davis spoke, and he nodded in agreement at the end. "The meeting is in order and the motion is—"

"But what about J. P.?" Stanton interrupted. "It seems to me this is something that could wait a few days."

"You forget this is the last week of school," Condon said evenly. "In view of that fact, and since we have a quorum, I believe we should proceed. Your motion is acceptable, Jerry, and we'll consider it the first order of business. Any discussion?"

There was a lot of discussion—and opposition. Stanton and Thomas battled so vigorously and so long that Condon finally agreed to table formal action if Rockwell's Big Reds won the state championship. But he insisted on the vote, and, as expected, the motion was carried.

After the vote had been recorded, Condon suggested that all discussions and the decision be kept strictly confidential.

"We'll see how the team comes out in the championship games," he said agreeably. "If they win, we'll forget about it until later in the summer."

Valley Falls High School was electrified! Final exams, prom dates, commencement details, the end of school, and the play-off championships caught everyone up in a whirl of enthusiasm.

Chip hurried into the Sugar Bowl that evening, stopping long enough to look over Petey's shoulder at the sports page of the *Post* for the pairings in the championship play-off games.

State Baseball Play-Offs
Valley Falls Meets Seaburg

Wednesday Morning

The Big Reds travel to University Tuesday afternoon to defend their state baseball championship. The champs will face Seaburg, winner of Section Four, in their first game, Wednesday morning. The locals are favored to win the opener chiefly because Coach Henry Rockwell has announced William "Chip" Hilton will start on the mound.

What Rockwell will do for a pitcher in the Friday game—if the opener is won—presents a real problem because Nick Trullo is still nursing a sore arm. When questioned concerning his pitching plans, the veteran coach quipped: "We're playing them one at a time!"

BLUEPRINT FOR REVENGE

Hilton is strong, in good form, and could undoubtedly pitch Wednesday and Friday. That would give Trullo three additional days to rest his sore arm and get ready for the final game, but Rockwell has never been known to deviate from his rule that a high school pitcher be given three days rest. He will probably start Robert "Soapy" Smith in the second game and hope for the best.

Should Valley Falls get by Seaburg Wednesday morning, the Big Reds will play the winner of the Edgemont-Clinton game Friday afternoon.

The complete pairings follow:

Salem II*
Thursday A.M. }
Rutledge IV _____

Friday A.M.
_____

Coreyville I*
Wednesday P.M. }
Bloomfield III _____

Saturday P.M.
Champions _____

Edgemont III*
Thursday P.M. }
Clinton I _____

Friday P.M.
_____

Seaburg IV*
Wednesday A.M. }
Valley Falls II _____   * *Sectional Champions*

"Some draw," Petey said. "The Seabees are tough!"

Chip smiled wryly. "They're all tough in a tournament, Petey," he said gravely.

"Who's gonna pitch Friday?"

"You read what Rock said—"

"That's no answer, Chip," Petey pleaded. "Seriously, what are you guys gonna do for a hurler on Friday?"

"What makes you think we'll be playing Friday?"

"Because you're pitching Wednesday!" Petey said stoutly.

Chip laughed. "Wish I had your confidence. Maybe Nick will be all right by Friday, Petey," he said hopefully. "He'd better be, or else—"

"Or else what?"

"Or else Soapy Smith!"

"No way!"

"Yes way!"

Petey kept pleading for more information, but Chip hurried back to the storeroom. There, John Schroeder, shuffling some papers at the desk, was absorbed in his work, and Chip slipped quietly down the steps leading to the basement. He had a lot of unpacking and stock work to do if the Sugar Bowl and Valley Falls Pharmacy were going to operate efficiently during the four days he'd be at State. That thought brought an ironic smile. He'd be back in Valley Falls Wednesday night if he wasn't sharp on Wednesday morning.

Doc Jones was everyone's friend. Maybe that was why he knew everything that happened in Valley Falls just about as soon as it occurred. Undoubtedly, his close friendship with some members of the school board was responsible for the "confidential" information he shared with Schroeder in the storeroom a few minutes after Chip had started work.

"John, guess what I just learned?" Doc blurted out.

Chip smiled when he heard Jones's rasping voice. He had no interest in eavesdropping, but there wasn't much he could do about it. Chip heard the creak of the chair as Schroeder swung around. As Jones continued, Chip's smile vanished and his face hardened.

"The board voted for Rock's retirement at the end of the term. What do you think of that?"

"Oh, now, Doc, that can't be right! Someone's pulling your chain."

"No, John, I got it straight from Stanton. Condon forced it through at a special meeting today—vote was three to two. Ohlsen wasn't there!"

"You sure Stanton wasn't pulling your leg, Doc? Why, it's impossible!"

"It's not impossible, and Stanton wasn't kidding. He was dead serious and pretty sick about it. In fact, he and Trish are planning to resign. They're just waiting for Ohlsen to get back in town."

"Can't believe it!" Schroeder shook his head. "No one's worried about Rock's age! He's younger than many thirty-somethings I know."

"He's that, all right. It's not age. It must be young Davis and Cantwell and that crew. They've been after Rock for a long time. Never thought they'd ever get any support though. Oh, Jim said they did get Condon to say he'd hold everything off if the baseball team won the state tournament."

"He'd better," Schroeder said grimly. "If Rockwell brings back the championship after all the trouble he's had this year, this town will *give* him the high school. Personally, I think Condon's looking for trouble. People are getting fed up with him, his crowd, and his political games. About time too! You can tell it isn't an election year."

Jones grunted. "You can say that again," he said grimly. "The kids opened a lot of eyes in this town. You going to the meeting? Well, come on then. We're late."

Long after Schroeder and Jones had departed, Chip sat on the box he'd been unpacking, elbows on knees and chin in hands. Chip's mind was filled with a thousand bitter thoughts, all confused and all revolving around the shocking news he'd just overheard. Long minutes later when he'd gotten to his feet and back to work, he was still thoughtful but no longer confused. Now Chip Hilton and the Big Reds had something else to fight for in their championship quest at State.

Valley Falls gave the Big Reds a real send-off, lining the sidewalks from one end of Main Street to the other to cheer the red-and-white decorated bus on its way. The school band, one hundred strong, led the way. Petey hadn't forgotten his usual treats and came tearing out of the Sugar Bowl with a big box of burgers, chips, drinks, and fruit.

"Bring it back again!" he shouted. "We'll be waiting up Saturday night!"

Then they were on their way, singing and cheering. Valley Falls and all the troubled, doubtful days the team had experienced fighting to stay in the sectional were forgotten—forgotten to all of the players in that happy bus except Chip Hilton. Chip was listening and laughing with the rest, but his mind was busy thinking about Coach Rockwell. He nudged his seatmate.

"How's your arm, Nick?"

The big southpaw grimaced, pulling his lips into a tight line. He shook his head doubtfully. "It doesn't feel too good, Chip," he said in a low voice, "but it'll be all right when I need it. It's got to be all right! I've got to win one of those games. You can win the other two. Don't worry, I'll be all right!"

Buck Adams and Peck Weaver had been among the crowd of baseball fans lining Main Street. After the bus passed from sight, they strolled gloomily down the street, headed for Mike Sorelli's poolroom.

"We didn't do so good," Peck said sourly. "We better give it up!"

Adams grunted angrily. "I never give up! I started out to get those two, and I'm gonna do it!"

"How?"

"Don't know yet."

"Well, you'd better think of somethin' quick. They're playin' Wednesday morning. Hey, there's Waters and Davis. Hi ya, Jerry. Hey, Muddy. How ya doin'?"

"OK," Davis said shortly. "Looks like you two failed, all right."

"We're not through," Adams said aggressively. "Not yet!"

"Hope you're right," Davis said thoughtfully. "Confidentially, Rockwell's going to be tossed out on his ear if he doesn't bring the championship back."

Adams stopped in his tracks. "You mean that?" he asked, looking from Davis to Waters.

Davis's pale blue eyes were hard and cold, and his voice grated angrily. "Sure do," he said harshly. "Well, see you at State."

"You won't see us," Adams growled. "But if what you said is straight, you can bet Rockwell won't be around here next year!"

Adams and Weaver spent the rest of that afternoon and most of the evening trying to figure out what they could do. As usual, it was Buck who came up with the answer. It was beautiful in its simplicity.

"Look, Peck," he said triumphantly, "all we've got to do is get that kid's signature on a phony contract—"

"Oh, sure!" growled Weaver. "Would you mind tellin' me how we're goin' to—"

"Leave that to me. I got an idea. And when we flash that contract around the night before Hilton's s'posed to pitch, the sports reporters'll go to work, and Rockwell's pet will be out of there—but good!"

"I don't get it," muttered Weaver doubtfully.

Adams's shrewd and fertile imagination was clicking. Impatiently he explained, "Don't you get it, you idiot? It's simple! All we gotta do is get someone to go to the university and get Hilton's name on a bogus contract, show it to a couple of sportswriters, and we're in! And pretty boy's out! Get it?"

"Yeah, I guess so," Weaver said uncertainly. "But who you gonna get to do the job? It's gotta be a stranger, someone Hilton doesn't know and someone the sportswriters don't know. Some guy they'll never see again."

"Right! And I know just the guy! Donnie Delson!"

Weaver nodded doubtfully. "Yeah," he agreed reluctantly. "Donnie might be OK if you can keep him sober— and if you don't pay him off until the job's finished."

The State Athletic Association was a powerful organization, backed up by the administrators of every high school in the state, as well as by the state legislature. It was a generous and hospitable organization. When it sponsored a state tournament, the members of the organizing committee made sure the athletes, coaches, and their teams were treated right.

The University Hotel and Convention Center was housing all eight teams and many of their fans. When the Big Reds arrived, the lobby, the adjoining restaurants, the coffee shop, and the sidewalk outside were jammed with a milling crowd of happy ballplayers, coaches, parents, and supporters. The team's arrival was greeted boisterously.

"Here comes the reigning state champs!"

"Hey there, Big Reds, hey!"

"Better not unpack—we're sendin' you home!"

"Yeah, you won't be here long!"

"No championship for you guys this year!"

"Where's that trophy? You bring it back for us?"

It was all good-natured fun, and the Big Reds liked it. They even tossed out a few comebacks themselves. An athlete couldn't be blamed for lifting his chin a little higher and squaring his shoulders when he was on a championship club. The Big Reds even looked like champions. Each team member was neatly dressed and walked with the quiet confidence of a successful athlete.

After checking in and enjoying a team dinner, they mingled in the crowd, greeting old friends and making new acquaintances. Still, each Big Red kept his eye on the big grandfather clock in the lobby, and at nine o'clock every member of the squad assembled in Rockwell's room.

"Now, if we can get by tomorrow and Friday, we'll have Chip for the championship game. That is, if Nick can work Friday and get by—"

"He'll get by! He can do it!" the guys chorused.

"I'll work," Nick growled. "I'd like to see someone stop me!"

"You'll work if your arm's OK, Nick," Rockwell said firmly. "Your arm's more important than ten championships. Now, we'll take our team walk, and when we get back, it's lights out. All of us! By this time tomorrow night, we'll either be on our way home or planning the Friday game. Let's go!"

CHAPTER 14

Grand Slam

THE VALLEY FALLS bus turned left with the wave of the officer's arm and rolled up the smooth road lined on each side by stately red brick buildings covered in ivy. Chip scarcely noticed the beautiful green-carpeted campus; instead, his eyes focused on the top of the tall grandstand rising above the concrete wall extending away from the field house. And his heart was thumping when he jumped out of the bus in front of the players' entrance to the field. The usual pregame emotion gripped him, numbing the arm and hand carrying his traveling bag and turning his legs to rubber.

Memories of Seaburg High School flooded Chip's mind. The first game he'd ever pitched as a starter had been against the Seabees, and he'd come out of that game with a no-hitter. He smiled at the reminiscence. Most of the guys who'd played for Seaburg last year were back, including Thornton, the Seabees' star hurler he'd beaten that day. Chip had a hunch he'd meet Thornton head-on again today.

GRAND SLAM

Chip's hunch was right. When he trotted through the tunnel and out on the field, the first Seabee he saw was Thornton, who was warming up in front of the Seaburg dugout.

When Chip toed the warm-up rubber and heard the scattered cheers and yells from the Valley Falls stands, his mind and every muscle of his body were consumed with one thing and one thing only—the game.

Before he knew it, hitting and fielding practice was over, and he was sitting in a corner of the dugout wearing his red-and-white warm-up jacket. Out on the hill, Thornton was blazing them in, and Chip knew he had a fight on his hands. Thornton was in top form.

The Big Reds, batting first, didn't get far that inning or in the five innings that followed. Thornton was fast, and his control was perfect. Chip pitched his heart out, calling on his fastball, his slider, and his change-up to hold the Seabees scoreless for the first five innings. Each team had been able to muster only a few scattered singles.

Chip knew he was tiring. He needed a run or two for a cushion, so instead of continuing into the dugout when he came in for the top of the sixth, he stopped and waited for his teammates. As he stood there, it seemed as if all the Big Red fans had the same idea; this was it! The big end of the batting order was up and now was the time. The Valley Falls fans began beating the bleachers. The rhythmic stomping of their feet and the roar of their voices flooded the field, demanding the big rally.

Cody Collins led off, spreading his stubby legs in a wide stance, vigorously thumping his bat on the plate. Cody knew how to work a pitcher, crouching and bobbing and weaving like a boxer until the strike zone seemed no larger than the catcher's glove. Thornton didn't like it. He tried too hard to strike out the aggressive little batter and lost the battle of wills by giving up his first pass of the game.

With one on and none down, Speed Morris was up. Speed took a called strike, a ball, and then dropped a perfect bunt to the right of the plate. The catcher, Thornton, and the Seabee first baseman all converged on the ball; but because each hesitated, waiting for the other to field the ball, there was no play at all, and Cody and Speed were both safe.

Red Schwartz marched up to the plate next, swinging his favorite aluminum bat, eager to park one over the fence. But Rockwell had his two fastest runners at first and second, and Red followed the signs with a bunt right in front of the plate. The Seabees' receiver pounced on the ball like a cat, but Cody and Speed had exploded off the bases with Red's pivot, and Cody slid into third in a cloud of dust before the ball smacked into the third sacker's glove. The bases were loaded with nobody down.

The Valley Falls stands really let loose then, sending wave after wave of cheers across the field, drowning out the Seabee shouts as though they were whispers. Chip was on his feet yelling with everyone else when Biggie Cohen stepped into the batter's box. He was still yelling seconds later when the Big Reds' first baseman trotted across the plate following a grand-slam homer. Biggie had come through!

Thornton regained his tempo and set the next three batters down, but Valley Falls had a four-run cushion. It was all they needed. Chip retired the Seaburg hitters one-two-three in the bottom of the sixth and then again in the seventh. The Big Reds were in the semifinals!

That evening in the hotel, Chip called his mom and then joined Biggie and Soapy downstairs. The lobby and the surrounding shops were mobbed with groups of athletes with tanned faces, all talking and laughing and brimming over with baseball.

Competition for baseball talent is keen, and this tournament attracted a full complement of university and major league scouts and sports reporters. In the main restaurant, scouts, some wearing school and team logos, sat at several tables talking about old friendships and new talent. Underneath the pleasantries and joking there was plenty of serious thought. As the tournament players were discussed, each scout cocked an ear for information that might help him confirm his own opinions.

"What d'ya think of that Hilton kid?"

"Solid! Got a lot on the ball!"

"Lots of kids throw hard," someone drawled. "I didn't see his change-up."

"Change-up?" another snorted. "What's he need a change-up for? He's fast, and he's got control! Even you could teach him a change-up in a week! The kid's good!"

"Maybe he didn't show his change-up," someone suggested.

"I like that other kid," another voice broke in. "Thornton."

"I go along with that one. He mixes up his pitches and keeps the hitters guessing."

"He's curve-happy. You saw what that big lefty did to one of his hanging curveballs."

That's the way it went, each scout expressing his views, sometimes exaggerated and sometimes understated.

Later, the reporters and scouts converged on the lobby and mingled with the kids. Many of the high school players had received letters from universities or major-league organizations. Some of the players and their coaches had been contacted several times during the season, and most of the scouts were well known. Chip knew Stu Gardner, of course, but practically all the others were strangers to him—not that he didn't know them by reputation. Some were national figures and had been featured in sports magazines and papers all over the country.

Rumors had been flying all day about which players the scouts were most interested in, and Chip was glad his name was prominent on the list. Not that it meant he was interested in an immediate big-league career; college was his first objective, and he'd already completed his paperwork for State. Just the same, it made him feel good.

Stu Gardner saw Chip, Biggie, and Soapy and joined their little circle. Gardner was smiling. "Nice going, guys," he said happily. "You look like the class of the tournament to me!"

Soapy winked and nodded his head. "You tell 'em!" he said, smiling broadly. "We'll kill 'em! You see Biggie lay into that one in the top of the sixth? He hit it so hard it needed a new ZIP code when it came down! And how about the way Chipper, here, mowed 'em down? I tell you, we'll kill 'em!"

Everyone within hearing distance broke into laughter at Soapy's dramatics. In just two short days Soapy's "We'll kill 'em!" had become as well known as his flaming red hair in the coaching box and behind the plate. The burst of laughter drew attention to the group, and several reporters and scouts worked their way in their direction. The circle expanded until it filled the center of the lobby, the players intently asking questions while the scouts and sportswriters obligingly answered with behind-the-scenes stories of the major leagues and university ball.

GRAND SLAM

Chip was gradually crowded to the outer edge of the circle. Finding it difficult to hear, he moved over to a large window by the street and sank down in one of the leather chairs. He was soon so absorbed in watching the people passing by and wondering about their personalities that he was startled by a man's voice saying, "What are you doing over here all by yourself?"

Chip turned and glanced up quickly. The speaker was a tall, friendly man who Chip recognized as Perry Crane, a scout for the Eagles. Chip had read articles about him in the *Sporting News*. He had the reputation of being one of the most respected scouts in the game.

Without waiting for a reply, Crane sat in the chair next to Chip and stretched his long legs out comfortably. Then he extended a broad, suntanned hand. "My name's Perry Crane and I'm with the Eagles. Saw you work today. Nice throwing!"

Chip smiled as he shook Crane's hand. "Thank you, Mr. Crane," he said hesitantly. "I had more than my share of luck, I guess. Biggie sure saved us today."

"Been lucky a lot of times in the last couple of years," Crane grinned, "judging from your record. Today was the first time I ever saw you work. Not that I haven't heard about you," he quickly added. "By the way, what are you planning to do after graduation?"

"I plan to go to college at State, Mr. Crane," Chip said slowly, watching the scout's face anxiously. "That is," he continued, "if everything works out all right."

Crane smiled warmly. "Everything will work out all right," he said, nodding his head and tapping Chip on the chest. "Everything will work out just the way you want it—if you want it badly enough! That's one of the wonderful things about this great country of ours—people can do almost anything they set out to do, providing it's honest and they are honest in their desires and are willing to pay the price in study and work. Why . . ."

For the next hour Crane talked to Chip about the young athletes he'd met, about those who'd jumped at the opportunity to play pro baseball, and about those who'd chosen another profession. He lauded Henry Rockwell for the coach's contention that student-athletes could profit by college and should continue their education.

"More and more every year," he said, "college players are going into the major leagues. College kids get good coaching, and they're still young when they finish their degrees. A college education also gives them a good background for other opportunities in life."

Crane then described life in professional baseball—the downsides and the rewards. But not once did he attempt to discourage Chip's college ambitions.

Long after Crane had departed, Chip sat thinking about baseball and the men who were responsible for making it such a great game. He was proud he'd met Stu Gardner and Perry Crane and had been coached by a man like the Rock. Now, just when his high school career was ending, he understood many of the things that had puzzled him during the four short years he'd played for Valley Falls High School—like the Rock's emphasis on discipline and training and the importance of academics. Lots of the guys had thought Rockwell's constant barking about the importance of schoolwork was because he and the team might be deprived of a player's participation if he became ineligible. Chip had known better then, and he knew better now; he knew that the interests of a real coach, a coach like the Rock, extended far beyond a game, a season, and even a championship.

Thinking about Coach Rockwell, Chip glanced at his watch and sprinted for the elevator. The coach had called a team meeting for nine o'clock. He was ten minutes late!

It was so quiet when Chip paused outside Rockwell's door that he was sure he had the wrong room number. When he cautiously turned the knob and opened the door, he received a warning battery of eyes from his teammates and a cold glare from Henry Rockwell, but that was all. Rockwell continued his rundown of Clinton's batting order and then discussed strategy that might get the Big Reds past the semifinals and into the championship game. At ten o'clock, Valley Falls's Reds baseball champions, en masse, strolled along the familiar sidewalks at University for fifteen minutes and then went to bed full of baseball, confidence, and determination.

Baseball was the chief topic that evening in Valley Falls too. Stan Gomez's play-by-play coverage and Channel 10 Sports highlights had relayed the Big Reds' victory over Seaburg. Buck Adams and Peck Weaver had heard the broadcast, and for the first time that year they were in a happy mood.

"We're in," Adams said jubilantly. "Now all we want is for Trullo to win Friday afternoon."

"But what if Trullo loses?" Weaver objected.

"So what? That'll put Valley Falls out and Rockwell out, and that's what we want, isn't it?"

"Yeah, but how about our bets?"

"Forget the bets. We're out to get even with Rockwell and Hilton. Anyway, we won't bet until the championship game. Everything's perfect! We'll pick up Delson Friday morning and drive him to the university and have him do his thing Friday night. Saturday morning Rockwell won't know what hit him!"

CHAPTER 15

Signed, Sealed, and Delivered

CHIP WAS grinning happily when he finished the cover page of the fax to his mom. Then he reread for the tenth time the newspaper clipping he was sending along in the fax. The past two days had been exciting and eventful, and he was reluctant to lose any part of the memory.

Salem Meets Valley Falls
for Championship
Section Two Contenders Meet in Title Game Tomorrow

Underdog Valley Falls High School ball club, handicapped all season by injuries and a two-man pitching staff, fought an uphill battle yesterday afternoon to defeat Clinton High School by a score of 9-8.

Nick Trullo, the Big Reds' ailing number two hurler, was hit freely, but the support of his teammates was sensational. Time and again clutch plays saved the day. It was the seventh inning two-base pinch hit by Hilton that sent Cohen, the Valley Falls cleanup

SIGNED, SEALED, AND DELIVERED

hitter, in with the winning run. With two down in the bottom of the seventh, Clinton ahead 8-7, and Schwartz and Cohen on first and second respectively, Coach Henry Rockwell sent Hilton in to hit for Badger. The tall, rangy hitter pulled a screaming liner across the first-base bag and clear to the fence, scoring Schwartz and Cohen and breaking up the game.

For the first time, two baseball teams from the same section have won through to the finals. Salem, as expected, outhit and outscored Bloomfield in the morning semifinal, 8-2.

Salem won the Section Two championship by winning 14 of a 16-game schedule, while Valley Falls barely got under the wire ahead of Steeltown to win the runner-up spot with an 11-4 record. The ace hurlers of each club, Salem's Rick Parcels and Valley Falls's Chip Hilton, are slated to start. Hilton bested Parcels twice during the regular season to give Salem their only setbacks and that fact has established the Valley champions as the favorites.

The duel between these two pitchers will highlight the most successful championship series in the history of the State High School Athletic Association.

In addition to the five thousand fans, many college and major-league scouts will be in the stands for the two o'clock game. Talent galore will be on display.

Heading the stars are two of the state's leading hurlers, Hilton and Parcels. Outstanding infielders from both teams include Salem's hot corner flash, George Curry; Valley Falls's speedy shortstop, Speed Morris; and the Big Reds' hard-hitting first baseman, Biggie Cohen.

Salem undoubtedly has the greatest outfield ever to play in a state series. Antawn Hartman, Liam Shea, and Donnell Erickson are fast, good throwers and long-ball hitters. The edge in the receiving department goes to the Sailors because no one in the state can match the savvy and throwing ability of Vaughn "The Arm" Overton.

The hotel concierge promised to send out the fax immediately. Chip glanced at his watch. It was 6:45 and he had plenty of time. But he'd forgotten about the jammed lobby. It had never been so crowded as this, and, as he elbowed his way through the throng, he was greeted from all sides.

"Hi ya, Hilton! How's the arm?"

"Hey, Chip! Wait a minute!"

"What's the rush? Where you goin'?"

Chip tried to explain he was in a hurry, but that made no impression on the boisterous teenage athletes. They kidded him unmercifully.

"Bookstore? Better take a bodyguard!"

"Yeah, Salem's gonna kidnap YOU!"

"Got any insurance on that pitching arm?"

"How about an autograph?"

"Yeah, sign mine too! I'm from Salem!"

Chip took the good-natured kidding and grinned as he slowly made his way toward the shopping arcade. Then the crowd parted as Biggie came rolling through. Soapy and Red followed in his wake, and Chip fell in behind the trio. Suddenly, someone grabbed him by the arm.

"Excuse me. Ain't you Chip Hilton?"

Chip turned to face a middle-aged stranger. The man was carelessly dressed, and his face was flushed as he fumbled in his pocket.

"I . . . er . . . my kid's one of your fans, and I promised him I'd get your autograph. He's sick and—wait'll I get my pen . . . Here, you can sign this paper. It's all I got.

SIGNED, SEALED, AND DELIVERED

Wish it was a contract. Haven't signed one yet, have you? Well, if I was one of them big scouts, I'd sure want your name on my contract. Some joke, eh? That's right! Right there! Thanks a million! Good luck tomorrow!"

"He was sure in a hurry," Biggie drawled. "No one ever gets that excited over my autograph!"

"That's nothing," Soapy said ruefully. "No one even asks me for mine!"

"Maybe they know you can't write," Biggie joked.

The man was gone before Chip realized he was still holding the pen. He started after the stranger, but he'd disappeared in the crowd.

"I couldn't find him. Does it look expensive?" Chip asked.

"Don't worry about the pen. He knows where to find you if he wants it back," Red remarked.

"You're right. Let's get to the bookstore before it closes at seven. I want to get that book for my mom."

A few blocks away, Adams and Weaver waited impatiently in a parked car still unsure of Donnie Delson's dependability.

"Did you give him any money?" Weaver demanded.

Adams laughed shortly. "Do I look stupid?" he asked irritably. "He gets his money when the job's finished. Gettin' the autograph's the easiest part of the deal. Big thing's to fool the writers. Make them think he's legit."

"Yeah," Weaver agreed. "He'll hafta be good. Those sportswriters could be tough. Think he can do it?"

"Wouldn't be here if I didn't," Adams countered. "Delson's smart enough, all right, but I'm not too sure he looks the part."

"The local reporters for these games don't know the scouts," Weaver said. "Anyway, have him play up to one of the locals." He nudged Adams excitedly. "Here he comes now!"

Delson quickened his pace as he approached the car, then opened the back door and slumped down in the seat.

"Get it?" Adams demanded.

"Sure," Delson said casually, pulling the paper from his pocket. "It was easy!"

Adams unfolded the paper and looked at it closely. Adams thought it was an impressive looking document. At the top of the first page "contract" was printed in large letters. "The Chicago Bisons Baseball Club" completed the heading. On the signature line, written in ink, was the name Chip Hilton.

Buck turned and slapped Delson on the knee. "So far so good," he nodded. "I'll just sign for Mary Hilton and then we'll get goin'. Now comes the tough part. First, you're gonna wear one of my suits and go through a little rehearsal. That's why we checked into a motel away from the baseball crowd. Get goin', Peck!"

Donnie Delson wasn't a bad-looking man, and he had a pretty good heart. Unfortunately, he was an alcoholic, and Peck and Weaver were only too willing to take advantage of Delson's desperate need for money to feed his relentless illness.

An hour later Adams and Weaver surveyed him critically and then grunted their approval.

Weaver chuckled. "You look sharp, kid," he said admiringly.

"He's gotta do more than look sharp," Adams warned. "Now listen . . ."

They spent the next hour rehearsing Delson's every move, and it was ten o'clock before Adams was satisfied. "Let's go," he said tersely. "We don't have much time."

SIGNED, SEALED, AND DELIVERED

It wasn't difficult to locate the local sportswriters. Every night they joined the scouts and talked baseball. Like the scouts, writers talked to the players and the coaches, getting leads for special articles and swapping stories with everyone they met.

It took Delson nearly an hour to infiltrate the baseball group and another half hour to maneuver close enough to one of the local writers to strike up a conversation. All the time, he kept shuffling several index cards, as though they were playing cards. Adams had written the names of the outstanding players on these cards, and Delson kept adding little notes on some, crossing out others, and occasionally wadding one and tossing it over his shoulder. Curiosity finally attracted Jimmy Turk, a local sportswriter, just as Adams had planned.

"That the way you keep track of your prospects?" he asked.

"Yeah, that's one way," Delson replied.

"Who do you like?"

Delson shuffled the cards quickly, noting the numbers Adams had placed in the corner of each card. "Well," he said cautiously, "I've got my eyes on several of 'em. Here's a good prospect—name's Thornton, a pitcher—"

"You're interested in pitchers?"

Delson pursed his lips and eyed the questioner steadily. "Yeah," he drawled, "that's chiefly what I'm interested in—pitchers."

"Seems to me you've missed the best one."

Delson shook his head. "Not me!" he said shortly. "Look, I don't know what your game is, but mine's baseball. And particularly pitchers. I don't miss nobody!"

"What about that kid from Valley Falls? The Hilton kid?"

Delson eyed his companion suspiciously. "What about him?" he asked.

"He's the best young pitcher I ever saw."

Delson grinned. "Yeah, he ain't bad," he admitted cautiously, "not bad at all."

Turk laughed derisively. This guy must be crazy. Hilton was the best prospect he'd seen in years. He'd been so impressed he'd asked Chip to sign his souvenir program. He elbowed Delson. "Not bad," he repeated, "I'll say he isn't! Why, every scout in town is after him!"

Delson laughed and smiled mysteriously. "Won't do 'em no good. They're wastin' their time!" Delson paused, studied his prey carefully, and then continued abruptly. "I could let you in on a big secret if I was sure you wouldn't say anything about it until after the championship game."

Jimmy Turk was ambitious. He believed he could become a big-city sportswriter, and he was always looking for that one big story he could break that would make his career. He sensed this mysterious baseball scout's "secret" meant a scoop, and he quickly reassured Delson.

"Don't worry about that."

Delson played his part perfectly. He glanced covertly around and then edged closer to Turk. Cautiously pulling the contract out of his pocket, Delson carefully fumbled the front page just long enough for Turk to pick out the key words "Bisons" and "contract." Then Delson placed a finger under Chip's signature and tapped the "Mary Hilton" underneath.

"Signed, sealed, and delivered," he gloated. "Is that a secret or is that a secret? Guess you understand now what I meant when I said a lot of guys were wastin' their time. 'Course we ain't gonna do no formal announcin' until the kid graduates, but he's signed tight enough. Get it?"

Turk got it all right, and his thoughts were racing. Here was the break he'd been waiting for, the scoop of the tournament, maybe of the entire year. He could scarcely restrain his excitement. He was anxious to get away and write the story, but he exercised a bit of caution. Fortunately, he reflected, he'd gotten Chip Hilton's autograph just for fun, and he pictured the signature he'd seen on the contract in his mind. He pulled the tournament program out of his pocket and carelessly turned the pages until he came to the Valley Falls section.

His heart leaped. The signatures were identical. There was no doubt in Turk's mind now. This was the scoop to end all tournament scoops, and it was all his, provided he could get this scout out of here before he told someone else about the contract. He shook his head in admiration. "Nice going! Every scout in town's been after that kid. Let's go get something to eat."

Delson shook his head. "No, thanks," he said, affecting a yawn. "I'm dead tired. Think I'll turn in. See ya later. Now, be sure to keep what I showed you to yourself until next week. The kid graduates Monday, and it'll be in all the papers Tuesday. That's for sure!"

A few minutes later, each was chuckling to himself as he hurried away. Turk wanted to get down to the office and get his story ready for the morning paper, and Delson wanted to report to Adams and collect his money. He'd made up his mind to have a real weekend for himself. Adams thought differently.

"No money," Buck growled. "No money 'til we see tomorrow morning's paper."

"But look, Buck," Delson pleaded, "I did my part. What's the idea? You said I'd get paid as soon as I contacted the reporter."

Adams shook his head. "Oh, no, Donnie," he said grimly. "I told you you'd get paid when the job was finished. That means when and if the story hits the paper."

"It'll hit the paper, all right! Come on, Buck," Delson pleaded. "Let me have some of the money."

"Nothin' doin'! You get paid in full tomorrow! We'll drop you off at the motel, and you stay in and sleep late. We'll meet you at two o'clock tomorrow afternoon as planned, and you'll get paid in full—plus a bonus, if the story gets the headline. Now gimme that fake contract."

Delson shook his head stubbornly. "Nothin' doin', Buck," he said sullenly. "You get the contract when I get paid."

After dropping Delson off, Adams headed back to University. As he drove through the deserted streets, he talked rapidly, half to himself and half to Weaver.

"Now we've got to do our part. First, we gotta check that guy Turk and make sure he's writin' the story. He oughta be at the newspaper office. Then we hit the right spots to make our bets on the game. You wait here in the car, and I'll go up there and pretend to be lookin' for somethin' in one of last week's papers."

"Still think you oughta call this Turk on the phone," Weaver said stubbornly.

Adams shook his head. "Nope," he said softly, "too risky. He might get suspicious. You stay here. I'll be right back."

A few minutes later Adams came scrambling back into the car. "OK, Peck," he said, "we're in! The guy's writin' the story right now! The security guard stopped me, and I asked if I could see one of last week's papers. He said there wasn't anyone up there but Turk, so I said forget it. Said I'd come back in the morning. Not! I'll be busy in the morning, but it won't be readin' one of last week's papers!"

"Hilton and Rockwell are gonna be busy too," Weaver crowed. "Busy tryin' to explain their way outta this one!"

"They might do it," Adams snickered, "but it'll be too late! Too late to win the game!"

CHAPTER 16

A Special Sports Story

STU GARDNER whistled under his breath and pressed the morning paper out flat on the counter, nearly upsetting the cup of coffee he'd been sipping.

"What's the matter, too hot?" the waitress asked.

"I'll say!" Gardner replied. "Too hot to be true!" He swung around on the stool and startled her by bolting for the door.

Gardner's feet were racing almost as fast as his thoughts as he dashed through the door of the hotel coffee shop. "Can't be," he muttered, heading for the elevator, "just can't be! Something's wrong!"

At that same moment, Soapy was shaking the morning paper in Chip's face. "Look, Chip! Look at this!" he shouted, jabbing a finger into the paper. "What's this all about?"

Chip, resting for the game, was half asleep when his startled eyes flashed from Soapy to the front-page headline. His first glance brought him to his feet, wide awake.

PITCHERS' DUEL

Valley Falls Pitcher Faces Eligibility Charge
Committee to Investigate Report of Contract Signing
A Special Sports Story
by Jimmy Turk

William "Chip" Hilton, brilliant pitching star of the Valley Falls baseball team, is reported to have signed a contract with the Chicago Bisons. Hilton was slated to pitch against Salem at two o'clock this afternoon in the final game of the state championship series.

Efforts to contact Hilton and Coach Henry Rockwell late last night were unsuccessful. Rockwell had left strict orders that neither he nor the Valley Falls players were to be disturbed.

Dr. Anthony Beldon, chairman of the State High School Athletic Association, reached at his home in Steeltown, stated he had no knowledge of this incident prior to this reporter's call but that the matter would be discussed at the luncheon meeting of his committee today here in University.

If the report is substantiated, Hilton will not be permitted to pitch in today's game. The eligibility provisions of the High School Athletic Association specifically state that a high school athlete who signs a professional sports contract before the day following his graduation shall be immediately and automatically ineligible for further participation in any and all high school sports.

Hilton has been the pitching sensation of the state for the past two years, and his brilliant performances have been followed by most universities and major league clubs in the country. Although rules prohibit scouts from contacting and signing a high school player until after his class has graduated, there are many loopholes in the provision. Hilton is such a prize that extreme efforts have undoubtedly been made to secure his services. The loss of the Valley Falls star . . .

Chip sank down on the side of the bed, his mouth agape, amazement written all over his face.

"We've got to see the Rock," Soapy growled. "Now! Hey," he said, pivoting, "any truth to this? Anyone try to sign you to a contract?"

Chip shook his head vigorously. "What do you think? Of course not! Come on! Let's go!"

Rockwell had been as surprised and bewildered as Chip. Holding the paper Gardner had thrust into his hand, Rockwell quickly scanned Turk's article while standing by the dresser in his room. He handed the paper back to the friendly scout.

"This is impossible, Stu! Chip would no more sign a contract without telling me about it than, than—why, who ever heard of such a thing?"

"Obviously, a guy by the name of Turk must have heard of such a thing," Gardner said dryly, tapping the paper.

"Maybe," Rockwell said grimly. "I'll call Chi—"

But Rockwell didn't have to call. Just as Rockwell began dialing, Chip knocked on the door.

As soon as he entered the room, Chip knew the two men had read the story.

"Chip, have you seen the morning paper?"

"That's why I'm here, Coach. Soapy just showed it to me. Coach, why would anyone write a story like that? It's not true!"

Rockwell turned to Gardner. "I knew it Stu," he said. "I knew it!"

Gardner nodded. "I knew it too, Rock," he said, "but this story's dynamite! You realize what time it is? It's eleven thirty and you're scheduled to play at two. You've got to get busy! The state committee meets at twelve and they may take action against Chip and Valley Falls!"

Rockwell bit off his words angrily. "Over my dead body," he said grimly. "I'll have something to say about that! I'd sure like to get hold of this guy Turk!" He turned to Chip. "You know him?"

Chip shook his head. "I never heard of him, Coach."

Rockwell spun around and grabbed the phone. "Room 514."

"Chet? Rock! Look, we've got a situation. You saw it? Well, then you know. Now listen! You and the team go ahead. I'll take Chip with me and check with the committee! Don't wait! Take your batting practice and infield workout and keep the kids focused! We'll be there as soon as we clear this thing up. What's that?"

"Smith!"

"But there isn't anyone else!"

"He's right here! Now get going! We'll probably be there as soon as you are. I'll clear this nonsense up in a hurry."

"OK! Good! Get going!"

Rockwell was all action now. He sent Soapy flying to join Stewart and then hurried away with Chip to meet the state committee. Stu Gardner wasn't idle either. He'd been trying to figure a way to help out. He didn't share Rockwell's confidence that the state committee could be handled so easily, and he was on the phone before Rockwell and Chip were on the elevator. It was unusual for a scout from one club to call another team office, but this was an emergency. Gardner liked Rockwell, and he liked the Valley Falls kids. If there was any way to clear up this mess and help Chip Hilton, Stu Gardner had made up his mind he was going to do it.

The whole thing smelled funny to him, and his voice betrayed his anxiety as he reached a weekend intern at the Bison office. "Call me back as soon as you reach either of them, will you, please? I'll talk to anyone! It's very important!"

Gardner sat down heavily on the bed and tried to figure it out. The Bison management didn't work this way. Stu was sure of that. He knew the Bison main office had never authorized a scout to sign any player before the deadline. And he knew them well enough to be sure that they'd tell him if any of the Chicago Bison scouts were here. He hadn't seen Bill Peterson or Rudy Miller. They were the top men in the Bison scouting organization. Maybe it was someone new. . . .

Stu was still clutching the paper. He glanced at the story again. "Jimmy Turk," he muttered. "I'll call him next! Mr. Turk's gonna have to do some fast talkin' to me!"

Gardner got immediate action on his call to the newspaper. "Everyone's gone for the day," the indignant voice advised.

"Where can I find Jimmy Turk?" Gardner asked.

"How do I know? Let your fingers do the walking! Don't you know this is Saturday?" The phone clicked in his ear.

Gardner leafed through the phone directory. No listing for Jimmy Turk. Then the phone rang.

The call from Chicago cut off another lead as the intern apologized. "Sorry, Mr. Gardner, the whole team is on a flight out west for a three-game series, and I can't reach anyone else you named."

Gardner knew eventually Jimmy Turk would be at the game; he was probably there already. Anyway, Stu

Gardner was going to find him. Grabbing his jacket, Stu left his room and headed for the front desk to order a cab. As the taxi followed the long line of cars heading for University Field, Stu was thinking about Rockwell and Chip and hoping they were having better success with the committee.

But they weren't making out at all! Dr. Beldon and the other members of the eligibility committee couldn't agree with the frantic Valley Falls coach. "You'll just have to understand our position, Coach Rockwell," Beldon was saying firmly. "In spite of what you say and as much as we want to believe William Hilton, here, we have no alternative but to keep him out of the game until we have proof of some kind."

Rockwell was livid. "You mean *that's* proof?" he demanded, pointing to the paper.

"Not necessarily," Beldon said slowly, "but it is a public statement and has been read by thousands of people this morning who are vitally concerned with the boys and the sports of this state. We've got to take some action. We'd be erring in our responsibilities if we passed it over without some evidence to disprove the assertions." He turned to Chip.

"Did you ever talk to a Bison scout, Hilton?"

Chip shook his head. "No, sir," he said firmly, "that is, not to my knowledge."

"Did you talk to any scout?"

"Oh yes, sir. Several, in fact."

"Was there an agreement of any kind? Verbal or otherwise?"

Chip shook his head vigorously. "No, sir. Never!"

"This is all nonsense!" Rockwell bellowed. "This young man has told you he never signed anything! What more do you want to know? I never heard so much nonsense in my whole life! How can he prove something that didn't happen?"

Nonsense or not, Beldon and his committee members were persistent. "Coach Rockwell, the reporter told me he saw the contract and identified your player's signature on the document."

Despite Rockwell's arguments, they stood their ground. Chip Hilton was ineligible to play and would remain ineligible until he could prove otherwise.

"But look at the time," Rockwell said impatiently. "It's one o'clock now, and the game starts in an hour. Where could we get any proof in that little bit of time? That's stupid! His word is as good as gold! I'd stake my life on it!"

Beldon assured Rockwell that he and his committee believed Chip, too, but further investigation was imperative. Then he eased the situation somewhat by telling the worried coach that Jimmy Turk had been assigned to cover the game for his paper and that the secretary of the state association was in the press box waiting for the sportswriter.

"We'll have Mr. Turk on the phone the minute he shows up, Coach," Beldon continued, "and we'll try our level best to get the facts."

"Facts!" Rockwell snorted. "Huh! That's a big help!"

Beldon glanced at his watch. "It's 1:15 now," he said soothingly. "Why don't you leave Chip with us and go on out to the game? As soon as we can get any information at all, we'll rush him to the field."

All the time Beldon had been talking, Rockwell had been striding back and forth across the room, muttering to himself. Now he stopped and faced Beldon, cold anger blazing from his eyes, his voice choked with emotion. "But I don't have a pitcher," he stormed. "What's the use of going out to the park?"

"I imagine your other players are upset too," Beldon said quietly. "Personally, I think your place is with them. You can't do much here."

Rockwell nodded his head vigorously. "You can say that again!" he said curtly. He deliberated for a moment and then started for the door. As he passed Chip, he placed both hands on the dejected player's shoulders and looked directly into his serious gray eyes. "I believe you. See it through, Chipper," he said softly. "We're all behind you."

At the door he stopped again. "We'll play the game," he said, his voice cold with repressed anger, "with or without Chip—but under formal protest! I'm advising you right now that you, the state athletic association, Jimmy Turk, and everyone else mixed up in this non-sense are going to rue the day you permitted some clown to keep this kid from playing in that game today. Mark my words!" The door banged and he was gone.

There wasn't a sound in the room after Rockwell slammed the door. Everyone appeared to be in deep thought. Chip was completely demoralized. He reviewed every minute of his stay at University, starting with the arrival of the team at the hotel Tuesday evening. At no time had any scout made him a proposition or asked him to sign a contract. Sign . . . Why, the only things he'd signed had been the hotel room service bill, his fax to his mom, and a few autographs.

Minutes later, the telephone rang and Beldon was talking to Turk. Chip could gather from the one-sided conversation that the sportswriter was firm in his con-victions and sure of his position. What in the world was this all about? He concentrated with all his might as Beldon talked.

"That's right! That's just what we want to know."

A SPECIAL SPORTS STORY

"You saw the contract with your own eyes?"

"And the two signatures were identical?"

"Did you know the scout?"

"You mean you don't know his name?"

"Would you recognize him?"

"Didn't you attempt to verify the story?"

"Of course I understand the time element! But how about the student-athlete? How about the ethical factors?"

"But what if you made a mistake? What if it was a joke? Or a set-up? Think what you may have done to this young man and his team."

"Well, you'd better be right! You have placed me and my committee and the State High School Athletic Association in a terrible position. I want you to know right now that if that story proves to be false, you and your paper are in for trouble. A whole lot of trouble! Your editor will be the first to hear from me."

"I'm afraid any help you can give us now is too late."

"All right, in the fieldhouse. Dr. Young's office will probably be best. We're leaving right now!"

When Rockwell arrived at University Field, the first person he met was Stu Gardner. Gardner searched the face of the worried coach, but what he saw there killed his hopes. "No luck, eh," he said sympathetically.

"No, Stu," Rockwell said wearily. "What a mess! You locate Turk?"

"Not yet, Rock, but I will. You go ahead with the team, and I'll keep you posted. The guy's gotta show up before long. Soon as I learn anything, I'll let you know. Where's Chip?"

Rockwell told Gardner about the committee's action and then hurried toward the diamond. The Big Reds were taking their fielding practice when Rockwell swung through the gate by the grandstand. The scoreboard clock registered 1:50.

Hustling along, out of uniform for a Big Red ball game for the first time in his coaching career, Rockwell almost made it to the dugout before he was recognized. Then some keen-eyed Valley Falls fan spotted him, and he was bombarded with questions from every direction.

"Hey, Rock, wait a minute. Is it true?"

"Where's Hilton? Where's Chip?"

"Who you gonna pitch?"

"What happened?"

But Rockwell merely waved and ducked into the dugout without a word. He was oblivious to the tumult in the stands and to everything except delaying the game as long as possible.

Stewart was hitting fungoes, but when he saw the glances passing between the kids, he dropped the bat and joined Rock in the dugout. One keen glance at Rockwell's face was all his loyal assistant needed.

"Everything all right?" Rockwell asked tersely.

Stewart shook his head. "Nothing's right," he lamented. "Look at 'em!"

Rockwell didn't need to look. He'd felt the uncertainty gripping the Big Reds as soon as he'd dropped down in the dugout and caught sight of their nervous warm-up. These kids had come a long way. Limited in number, handicapped with injuries, and shy of reserves, they'd fought for every run and every out through a precarious season—and the inspiration for that fight had come from their elected captain, Chip Hilton.

They'd lost easy games and had nearly fallen apart during Chip's unwarranted suspension, and Rockwell knew that without him today they might collapse completely. His keen black eyes caught the covert glances directed toward the dugout, and, in spite of his desire to delay the game as long as possible, he breathed a sigh of relief when they came trotting in and gathered around him in the dugout.

Every player there was thinking the same thing, but Biggie voiced the question. "Chip all right, Coach?"

Rockwell shook his head. "Not yet, but he will be! They're working on it now. He'll be here as soon as they check a few things."

"Chip wouldn't do anything like that!" Nick asserted.

Cody blasted. "Wouldn't? You mean *couldn't!* Isn't built that way!"

"We all agree on that, Cody," Rockwell said softly. "Now listen! We've got to go out there and fight as never before. Soapy, you start! You've got to hold them until Chip gets here! The rest of you get up on your toes and stay there! Give Soapy everything you've got. We beat them before, and we can do it again.

"We're first at bat, and we'll hit in this order: Collins, Morris, Schwartz, Cohen, Badger, Trullo, Peters—you'll be in right—Carey, and Smith. All right, Cody, start us out right! Carl, you and Soapy get out there at the end of the bleachers and get ready! All right—"

Rockwell's words were drowned by the clamor that greeted the umpire's announcement:

"Battery for Valley Falls: Smith, pitching; Carey, catching.

"For Salem: Parcels, pitching; Overton, catching.

"Play ball!"

The Blue Car

DR. ANTHONY BELDON had been active in the physical education and athletic programs of the state for many years, but he'd never experienced a situation like this one. Beldon had known and respected Henry Rockwell for most of those years, and now he felt as if he knew the young student-athlete sitting quietly by his side almost as well as he knew his mentor. It was a strange paradox, he was thinking, that you could work with a person much of your career and remain a stranger, while one hour spent with a new acquaintance could result in complete understanding and trust.

Chip Hilton was known all over the state for his athletic accomplishments, and Beldon knew his fine record almost by heart. Now he personally knew much more about this good-looking, gray-eyed teenager, which made what he had to do all the more difficult. Chip Hilton possessed real moral courage. His behavior and attitude in the face of this unexplainable situation had been admirable, and Beldon wanted so desperately to help Chip that he was almost running when he led the group up the steps and into the office of D. H. Young, State's director of athletics.

Stu Gardner was standing by the phone, and Jimmy Turk was sitting at a table nervously tapping his fingers. The strained silence in the office indicated their meeting had been anything but pleasant.

Beldon nodded shortly and came directly to the point: "Now, let's have the whole story, Mr. Turk."

Turk told them about meeting Delson, about the Bison contract, and about the signatures. He described his comparison of the signature on the contract with Chip's autograph on his souvenir program and then told how he'd tried to contact Rockwell and Hilton.

"I had to meet the morning deadline," he explained. "Otherwise, I would've had more time to work on the story."

"I'd think so," Beldon grunted. "Well, that leaves us exactly nowhere!"

"Not necessarily," Gardner interrupted. "Not if we can locate the man Turk talked to. By the way," he added, "my name is Stu Gardner, and I scout for the Drakes. I know just about every scout in the country. From the description Turk gave me, the man's an impostor. He doesn't sound like anyone I've ever met. I've got a call in now for Commissioner Burrows! Finally located him in New York."

Jimmy Turk was beginning to perspire. Insecurity mounted with each passing minute. He was beginning to realize just how serious this situation could be if he'd been duped. He would have ruined not only this kid's athletic career but also his own as a sportswriter. He had avoided Chip's eyes up to this moment, but now he felt he had to know Chip's reaction. "I don't want you to think I doubt you, Hilton," he began, "but how do you explain your signature?"

"I have no explanation for the signature," Chip said calmly. "You can hardly expect me to explain something I know nothing about. I do know, though, that I never signed a contract!"

"Signatures are easily forged," Gardner added dryly. "Where did you meet this 'scout,' Turk?" Beldon asked. "Maybe they know him at the hotel."

Turk nodded nervously. "They might," he said hopefully. "If I could talk to them—"

"That's easy enough," Gardner said curtly. "I'll get a cab!"

Beldon stopped him. "Not necessary," he said. "Let's take my car. Come on, Chip, you come along too. We may need you!"

Gardner elbowed Turk. "What about the game? How you going to get your story?"

Turk's eyes were hard. "It looks like this is going to be a better story. Besides," he said grimly, "I want to be in on this one to the finish!"

Just as they reached the outside steps, a tremendous roar exploded from the stands. Instinctively, their steps quickened. Chip and Gardner exchanged glances, but neither spoke. The cheer could mean everything or nothing, depending upon your seat in the ballpark.

Chip's heart and spirit sank. What was the use of all this? He ought to be on the bench . . . No! He ought to be out there pitching! For a brief second he almost hated Turk and felt like lashing out. Then he remembered his mom's counsel and conquered the sudden impulse.

The trip to the hotel was futile. No one knew or remembered seeing the man Turk described. Beldon was discouraged. "Looks like we're beaten," he said gloomily. "I guess we might as well go back to the game and wait for the call from Commissioner Burrows. I'm sorry, Chip. Personally, I'd give anything to be able to give you an OK."

Chip said nothing, but he swallowed hard as he looked out the window of the car. There went the last hope. Not another word was spoken as Beldon drove down Main Street toward University Road. Chip was still staring out the window, thinking about the game and wondering how Soapy was handling things.

Soapy wasn't handling things and hadn't been handling things from the start. He'd been in one hole after another, and now he was getting used to it. Parcels had set the Big Reds down one-two-three in the first inning, but Soapy had walked the first batter, hit the second, and loaded the bases with another walk. Only a sensational double play by Cody Collins and Speed Morris had pulled him out of that hole. As it was, the Sailors had scored two runs.

Then Soapy had looked at the clock and at the scoreboard and had started to stall. Every pitch became a complete act with Carl Carey cooperating beautifully. Carl would walk halfway out to the mound after each pitch, and Soapy would meet him. Carl would hand the ball to Soapy, slap him on the shoulder, and each would about-face and stalk slowly back to his position. Soapy would then pick up the resin bag, daintily dust his fingers, and nonchalantly toss the little sack over his shoulder. Next, Soapy would look at each of his teammates and wait for words of encouragement.

Then it would be Carey's turn. He'd have trouble with his mask, drop his catcher's helmet on the ground, loosen the strap on his glove, find a shoelace untied, and take time to brush a stray piece of clay from the plate. Squatting, finally, he would give the sign.

Soapy would then start the shake-off act. Carl would call for a fastball. Soapy would shake him off. Carl would show two fingers, and Soapy would ignore the call. Carl would give the sign for a knuckler, and Soapy would shake his head so vigorously his cap would fall off. Finally, Soapy and Carey would agree on a sign. In reality, signs meant nothing to Soapy. His only pitch was a straight ball—in the strike zone, when possible.

The fans and the umpires were amused at first, but when the Sailors began to complain, the plate umpire warned Soapy and Carey. He finally called Rockwell into a huddle with the two players. "You're allowed twenty seconds to put the ball in play—not forty," he advised Soapy. "And if you don't hustle up a bit, I'll start calling a ball every time you exceed the time limit. You've got to keep the ball in play!"

Soapy nodded gravely and proceeded to keep the ball in play. He threw to an occupied base at every opportunity. And he had lots of opportunities. It seemed that one or more Sailors were always on base. If the fielding and throwing of the Big Reds had not been sensational, the game would have been a farce.

In the fourth inning, with Salem leading 7-0, the top of the Big Red batting order came up. Collins led off and got on when Parcels issued his first pass of the game. With the hit and run on, Speed smashed a hard grass burner between the first and second baseman for a single, and Cody took third.

The Valley Falls fans sensed a rally, and their cheers mounted to one continuous roar. Then Red Schwartz met one of Parcels's fastballs right on the nose, blooping a single to right-center field. Collins scored, Speed went to third, and Cohen was up. Parcels did just what everyone expected him to do, intentionally walking Biggie to fill the bases, and that brought Badger to the plate. Chris kept the rally going and sent every Big Red fan into hysterics by driving the first pitch against the left-field fence. Before the rebound was fielded and returned to the infield, three more runs had scored and Badger was on third. But that was it. Parcels steadied, and Trullo, Peters, and Carey were easy outs, leaving Badger stranded.

The rally had given the Big Reds a lift, and they hustled out on the field for the bottom of the fourth only three runs behind. Then Soapy uttered a few silent prayers and resumed the stalling act.

Chip would've been thrilled if he could've seen that fourth inning rally, but at that very moment, he was experiencing another kind of thrill. Just as Dr. Beldon turned on University Road, Chip caught sight of a familiar blue car. The car was going in the opposite direction and was going so fast that it was almost out of sight before anything clicked. Then Chip came to life with a shout. "Stop! Turn around! Please! Hurry!"

Beldon was startled, but he reacted quickly, making a perfectly illegal U-turn. Chip was leaning out the window, his eyes focused far down the road. Then, just as Beldon's car roared ahead, the blue car turned right on Main Street.

Chip had lost all hope of making the game by this time. Now his only purpose was to get to the bottom of this mystery. Deep down in his heart he was praying for the Rock and the guys. "They've got to win," he muttered over and over. "Got to win for the Rock!"

They were nearly to the corner now. "Don't lose that blue car!" Chip pleaded.

"Why the blue car?" Gardner yelled. "You know the driver?"

Chip shook his head. "No, I didn't see the driver, but I know that car, and I think it's the answer!"

Chip leaned back out the window and then groaned. The light ahead flashed from green to yellow and then to red. Beldon saw it all right, but he didn't groan and he didn't stop. He leaned on the horn, punched the gas, and took the turn with screeching brakes and tires.

Gardner pointed ahead. "Turning left," he called. "Second corner!"

Beldon took his share of Main Street right out of the center and cut left at the second corner. There, half a block ahead, was the blue car.

"Slow down," Chip cautioned. "Don't let them know we're following."

The car ahead pulled up to the curb, and Beldon skillfully swung in behind a parked car.

Chip didn't say a word. He was watching the car like a hawk. Two men got out and entered the building.

Gardner muttered, "Now what?"

"It's them, all right," Chip declared. "It's Adams and Weaver! They're mixed up in this some way. I know it! We've got to follow them! They'll recognize me though."

"Well, they won't recognize me," Gardner said grimly. "Wait here! I'll be right back!"

Gardner walked into a veritable greasy spoon. A long, badly scarred, wooden counter extended along one wall. Behind it was a shelf holding the usual assortment of pasty-looking pies, cakes, and puddings. Several fly-specked mirrors served as a backdrop for the unappetizing display. On the other side of the room, separated from the counter by a number of small tables, several booths lined the wall. A small radio was blaring the championship game.

THE BLUE CAR

When Gardner entered, dropped down on a stool at the counter, and ordered a cup of coffee, Delson was arguing heatedly with Adams. Gardner had recognized Adams and Weaver as the men who'd gotten out of the blue car, but he didn't get a look at the third man. When he lifted the cup of coffee and caught a glimpse of Delson in the mirror behind the counter, he nearly choked. He gulped furiously and glanced away. If that wasn't the man Turk had described, it was a clone! He waited until the sports announcer gave the score before slipping a dollar on the counter and walking out.

Adams was trying to ignore Delson. "Shut up," he growled. "I want to listen to the game."

"Forget the game," Delson snarled. "I want my money. Now!"

"Chill out," Weaver said roughly. "You'll get paid! Don't you want that bonus? Hear that score? We're in!"

Weaver reveled. "Bottom of the fifth and Salem leadin' 9-4! We can't lose!"

"Come on, Buck," Delson pleaded, "pay me. I don't care about the bonus."

"Take it easy, Donnie," Adams mumbled. "We'll settle up just as soon as the game's over."

"You mean if that crazy Smith ever gets Salem out," Weaver sneered.

"Every run the Sailors get is just that much more insurance for us," Adams grinned. "Bases loaded again. Now ain't that just too bad!"

"Yeah," Weaver snorted. "Too bad for the Rockhead and Pretty Boy!"

"Look, Buck," Delson urged, "I'm shaking."

Adams pushed him roughly. "So what!" he snarled. "I told you I'd pay you as soon as the game was over. Go take a walk."

PITCHERS' DUEL

Gardner had forced himself to walk casually back to the car. "It's him!" he exulted. "I'm positive! It's the man we're looking for, and he's talking to those two other guys. Let's go get 'em!"

Beldon grasped the excited scout by the arm. "Hold it, Stu," he urged. "We can't afford to make a mistake! This is serious, and we need the police. Turk can identify the guy, but he'll have to be careful not to let the man see him. Chip, you stay here and watch! I'll call the police!"

CHAPTER 18

A New Ball Game

ROCKWELL WAS a fighter. Friends and enemies both agreed he never knew when he was beaten, and he never gave up. But as he sat in the dugout in the bottom of the fifth and saw Soapy working himself into another hole, it was all the veteran coach could do to resist a groan of despair. Salem was leading 9-4; there was no one out; two Sailors were aboard; and Soapy had just thrown one in the dirt to make the count three balls and no strikes.

The fans really got on Soapy then. They had laughed at and with him at first but had become impatient later because of his delaying tactics. They'd finally turned antagonistic when they realized that as a pitcher, all Soapy had on the ball were his fingerprints.

Still, Soapy kept trying, bravely stuck to his deliberate delivery, and took the taunts and jeers like a champion. Rockwell was suffering as much as Soapy, throwing every pitch with the affable teenager and feeling the bitter sting of every barb directed at the lovable redhead.

PITCHERS' DUEL

Things went from bad to worse, but Soapy kept fighting and trying. Rockwell felt a twinge of shame at his own weakness, and then his fiery aggressiveness came rushing back. He glanced along the bench before he realized that what he was doing was only wishful thinking. There just wasn't anyone on the bench. He called time and walked out to the mound to talk to Soapy. Cohen and Morris joined him there, and Nick Trullo came trotting in from the outfield.

Rockwell patted Soapy on the shoulder. "That's all right, kiddo," he said affectionately. "You're doing all right! How's your arm?"

Soapy swallowed before answering. "It feels all right, Coach, but I just can't seem to find the plate. You think Chip's gonna show up?"

"I don't know about that," Rockwell said grimly, "but I do know that a Big Red team never quits! Bear down, kid; we're with you! Come on, forget the crowd! They'll be cheering before this game is over!"

Nick Trullo touched Rockwell on the arm. "I feel great, Coach. Honest! Maybe if Soapy and I traded positions for a couple of outs—"

Rockwell shook his head firmly. "No, Nick," he said, smiling, "you worked yesterday. I won't take the chance—"

"But I'm not going anywhere in baseball, Coach. What does it matter? We want to win this one for Chip."

"I know, Nick," Rockwell said gently, "but you get back out there in left field." He turned to Soapy. "And you stay right in there, Soapy, and keep fighting! This game isn't going to be over until the last man's out!"

"Right, Coach!" Biggie gritted. "Come on, Soapy, we'll get to 'em sooner or later!"

Soapy grinned. He was his old self again. "Better make it soon," he said, waving his glove hand toward the scoreboard. "Now, what shall I do about this baby and the three-and-no count?"

Rockwell answered that question, biting off the words aggressively. "Throw a waste pitch and put him on! Then, you just take aim at the plate and let her fly. We'll do the rest!"

It worked. Soapy threw a wide one to fill the bases and, when the next hitter stepped to the plate, took aim and let the ball fly. The batter was late but met the ball solidly, sending a ground ball burning down the right-field baseline. Biggie dove for the ball almost with the crack of the bat, made a backhand stop, rolled over, and then threw from a sitting position for the force at home. That made it one away with the bases still loaded, but Soapy wasn't worrying. He took aim, let the ball fly again, and Rockwell's double-play combo did the rest. The batter drove the ball straight at Morris. Speed came in fast, took the ball neatly, and the double play was routine—Morris to Collins to Cohen.

Soapy was grinning widely when he dropped down into the dugout. "I'm gettin' the hang of it now," he quipped. "All you do is aim and let her fly! Wish Chip would hurry up!"

While this was going on, Chip was excitedly telling his listeners about Buck Adams and Peck Weaver and their feud with Rockwell. "They've been after Coach all year," he explained, "and when I saw Buck's blue car, I was positive they were in on this contract thing. They wanted us to lose bad! Guess they knew it meant Coach Rockwell's—" Chip bit his lip and stopped abruptly. He'd almost said too much.

"Coach Rockwell's what?" Gardner asked.

"Oh . . . er . . . that it meant so much to him," Chip answered lamely. There was a long silence.

Beldon had called the police, and, in spite of his hurry to get back to the car, dialed Young's office. An eager voice answered, and Beldon gave him the news.

"We've got 'em. Yes, the man who showed Turk the contract and two locals from Valley Falls who have it in for Rockwell! Have them cornered right now in a restaurant. Yes, I just called the police! The game over?"

Beldon listened anxiously. "Nine to four? I'm sure sorry to hear that. What's the inning? Top of the sixth? Looks as though we'll have to do something about Rockwell's protest! This is certainly a mess! Have Rockwell meet me in the office right after the game. We'll leave here as soon as the police arrive. Only good thing about the whole situation is catching this fake scout. How do I know he's a fake? Because I believe Chip Hilton! I'll call you back in a few minutes."

Jimmy Turk, sitting in the car, was just as deep in thought as Chip. He now knew he'd made a tragic mistake. This kid was too eager to find the man with the contract. If Chip had signed it, he'd be acting differently. "Now," Turk told himself, "you are in a predicament. Wait until I get my hands on that guy! He sure conned me! I fell for the whole deal—hook, line, and sinker! From what the kid says about these other two guys, it might be more than just a get-even stunt. What if it's connected to gambling ? I'd never live that down! Especially if Salem wins, and I don't see how they can lose with Hilton out of the game. If I get out of this one, I'll check, cross-check, and double-check every story I write the rest of my life!"

Turk would have been more than discouraged if he could've known how the game was going. Valley Falls had managed to tally another run in the top of the sixth, making the score Salem 9, Valley Falls 5. But that little ray of hope meant nothing. Soapy was already in trouble in the bottom of the sixth—and with the weak end of the Salem batting order, at that! With one down and Sailors on first and second, Overton, Salem's great catcher, was at bat.

"Hey!" Gardner's sudden explosion startled his companions. "Look who's coming out the door! Is that your scout, Turk?"

"It sure is!" Turk cried. "I'd know him a mile away! What are we going to do now? He's going in the other direction! He'll get away!"

"We've got to stop him," Gardner said fiercely. "We've got to hold him until the police get here!"

"I'll hold him!" Turk said abruptly. The sportswriter leaped out of the car and began running after the unsuspecting Delson.

Chip and Gardner could only watch. Turk sprinted down the street until he reached Delson's side and whirled the surprised man around. There was a brief exchange of words, and then Delson suddenly lashed out and knocked Turk to the pavement. Turk scrambled up on his hands and knees, trying to grasp Delson around the legs. But Delson backed away and kicked Turk solidly in the ribs before racing back toward the greasy spoon restaurant.

Just outside the door, Delson slowed his stride, started to enter, changed his mind, and finally ran in the direction of Beldon's car.

It all happened so quickly that Chip sat frozen in his seat, eyes glued on the advancing figure. As Delson came closer, Chip got a good look at the fleeing man's face and something clicked in his mind. He'd seen that man somewhere.

PITCHERS' DUEL

In no time Chip was out on the sidewalk and in full pursuit. Delson heard him coming and stopped, but Chip had already left his feet in a full-powered, head-on tackle. The two bodies crashed to the pavement. Chip clambered on top of Delson and pinned his shoulders to the ground. Then they recognized each other.

"The pen!" Chip gasped. "The autograph and the pen! Where's that paper you got me to autograph, you fake?"

Delson didn't answer but violently tried to regain his feet. Gardner stopped him, shoving Delson back to the sidewalk. Chip thrust his hand into Delson's inside jacket pocket, and there it was—the paper he'd autographed so innocently!

"So!" Chip exploded. "So you wanted my autograph for your sick son! Well, you got me out of the game, all right, but you got yourself into a deal that'll take you out of action too!"

"I'll say he did!" a strange voice boomed. "Let him go, young man. I'll take care of him now."

Chip looked up and was shocked to find he was ringed by a crowd of spectators. The speaker was a policeman, who promptly jerked Delson to his feet. Beldon arrived with a limping Turk as Chip scrambled up and handed the paper to Gardner.

Stu unfolded the crumpled paper and moved between Beldon and Turk. "So this is your idea of a major league contract?" he said sarcastically, holding the paper in front of Turk's face.

"By the way, do your eyes ever bother you? Take a good look this time! You ever see a letterhead? And you know what glue is? Well, someone pasted the Bison letterhead over the top of a standard apartment lease. Some contract! Some sportswriter! I hope this taught you a lesson!"

A NEW BALL GAME

Gardner shrugged contemptuously, turned away, and thrust the paper into Beldon's hand. "That satisfy you?" he demanded.

Beldon nodded. "Yes, Stu," he said quietly. "I've been satisfied ever since Chip told me it wasn't true. Right now, all I can say is that I'm sorry this happened and that I had to act as I did. You can be sure I'll do everything possible to rectify the mistake. But first, we've got to take care of this man's accomplices. Officer, they're in that restaurant!"

Beldon was wrong. Adams and Weaver were in the blue car driving swiftly back to the motel. They'd heard the commotion and rushed out just in time to witness Chip capture Delson. Adams muttered a curse, and he and Weaver headed, unnoticed, for the car.

Weaver was squirming and twisting. "That kid," he hissed angrily. "He always shows up! Now what are we gonna do?"

"First, we're gonna pack up and get out of that motel," Adams gritted. "As soon as that game's over, we're gonna collect our winnings and beat it! Oughta be over pretty soon. Find the game on the radio."

Top of the seventh now and Salem leads nine to five. Cohen is up. The big left-hander is Valley Falls's cleanup hitter. He's batting a thousand in this game, one for one; Parcels has walked the big first baseman twice.

Parcels won't give Cohen anything good, that's for sure! Here it comes; it's outside, one and no. The fans don't like it. They want to see Cohen hit. Parcels kicks, and Cohen swings. It's in there. It's good for a double! Hear that crowd! They love Cohen.

Rockwell's talking to the next hitter, Chris Badger, a great third baseman. This kid has a rifle arm from the hot corner and is two for three so far. His three-run triple in the fourth was right up against the fence.

Here's the pitch; it's in there for a called strike. Cohen's on second, staying close to the sack and taking no chances. Parcels delivers; Badger connects; it's on the ground between Curry and Aikin. Curry tries for it. He can't get it. It's a hit!

What a stop! Aikin went deep behind third base to get that ball. Oh, no! Cohen's caught between the bases! He's going back; there's the throw; it's going to be close; Cohen slides!

Well, the big guy got back, but it was close!

So with none gone, Cohen's still on the keystone bag and Badger's on first with Trullo at bat. Parcels kicks; Trullo swings, and it's a weak pop-up in the infield. The umpire calls the infield-fly rule and a dejected Nick Trullo walks back to the Valley Falls dugout.

That brings Peters up. He's the little southpaw who underwent an appendectomy last season and hasn't been used as a pitcher since. Rockwell could sure use another pitcher today. Rockwell's a stickler for protecting a kid's arm and health; otherwise, Trullo might be working today instead of Smith.

Peters isn't much of a hitter. Parcels has struck the little left-hander out three times in a row. Rockwell's talking to Peters; now he's at the plate.

Parcels throws; Peters pivots; he's going to lay one down. He does! Cohen and Badger are running. Parcels is in on the ball. Peters is going to make it! That kid can move. Parcels didn't even risk the throw.

That fills the bases. The tying run is at the plate, and Parcels calls time.

A NEW BALL GAME

Folks, that was one for the books. Smart, too. Salem—way out in front, playing deep and expecting Valley Falls to hit away—was crossed up.

This seventh-inning rally is dangerous. The ducks are on the pond. Now, don't go away. The score again is Salem 9, Valley Falls 5. There's one away, remember, bases loaded, and the tying run is at the plate—

Adams mouthed a curse. "Turn that thing off," he growled angrily. "Everything's goin' wrong on this deal!"

That's what Beldon was thinking too. Except for the man behind the counter, the restaurant was empty. The only sound in the place was the voice of the sportscaster on the radio. Beldon stopped short in utter astonishment, disbelief etched on his face as he listened.

. . . hit a grand-slam! This is really one for the books, folks! Soapy Smith—the Valley Falls catcher, turned pitcher for today's game because of Chip Hilton's eligibility difficulty—has just hit a four-run home run with two outs to tie up the score at 9-all here in the top of the seventh. It's a brand-new ball game!

CHAPTER 19

One Pitch!

CHIP'S HEART leaped. "A new ball game!" Before he could control his action, his head shot around and his hopeful glance met the steady gaze of Beldon's understanding eyes. Beldon smiled and nodded with enthusiasm, "Let's go!"

Beldon had hoped to corral all three men, and it was difficult for him to conceal his disappointment. From what he'd been able to gather, the two men who'd escaped were the ringleaders. The man they'd captured was not much more than a dupe himself. However, Chip's complete vindication and the good news from University Field now overrode everything but the game and getting Chip there as quickly as possible.

Beldon turned to the officer. "It looks as though they've gotten away, but I want to have charges brought against them. I'll come down to headquarters right after the game."

"If you don't mind, Mr. Beldon," Turk interrupted, "I'd like to press charges against them myself. I'm sure the paper will want to follow through on this, but whether it does or not, I certainly intend to do so. Besides, you're losing time, and I think Chip Hilton ought to have a chance to get into that game!"

Gardner exploded. "Get going, you two! I'll stay here and answer any questions the officers have."

Beldon and Chip were each impatient to get to the game. Chip had admired Beldon's driving skill in chasing the blue car, but he hadn't seen anything yet. Beldon hunched forward over the wheel, eyes picking out a path through the light afternoon traffic. Later, when Chip recalled that wild ride, he cringed as he remembered the close calls. At the time, however, he was conscious only that the car was speeding him to the game.

Events at University Field were making it appear doubtful that Chip would arrive in time to see the end of the game.

After Soapy's grand slam homer, Parcels had been so upset that he walked Collins. The brilliant Salem hurler had figured Smith would be tired; he tried too hard to strike him out, and the home run had been the result. Now, with the winning run on base, Parcels iced up and fanned Morris on three straight strikes.

Soapy took his time going out to the mound, trying desperately to figure out a way to slow down the game. He was watching for Chip so intently that he forgot to "take aim and let her fly," and as a result, he walked Parcels. There followed two infield outs on two sparkling plays. The Valley Falls fans began to hope. Unfortunately Soapy then fumbled Aikin's sacrifice bunt, putting runners on first and second, and Soapy promptly went to pieces, walking the Sailor second baseman, Burns, on four straight throws.

PITCHERS' DUEL

Carl Carey rifled the ball back to the mound so hard on the umpire's "ball four" that Soapy dropped it like a hot potato. Parcels, on third, broke for the plate, and only Biggie's alert recovery of the ball forced his return and kept the game from ending right there. With his teammates yelling encouragement, Soapy took aim and fired away. He got the count to three and two on Hartman, the Sailors' long-ball hitter. He took so long to look for the sign for the final pitch, however, that the umpire warned him, "Play ball or else!"

Carey squatted and started the usual routine with the sign for a fastball, but Soapy shook it off. He continued to shake his head as Carl went through every sign he knew and some he didn't. The umpire was just about to award Hartman a ball for Soapy's delaying when Carl called time and trotted out to the mound.

"What's the matter with you? What kind of sign do you want? What do you want to throw?"

"Nothin'!"

"What d'ya mean 'nothin'?"

"I just don't want to throw nothin'! Think I'm crazy? The bases loaded, last of the seventh, three and two on the batter, and the score tied! What d'ya mean, what do I wanna throw? I don't wanna throw nothin'! Ever again!"

That's where it stood when Chip and Beldon came running across the field. It was one of those unforgettable moments in baseball when the spectator becomes lost in the action and absorbed in the play, anticipating the climax. The spell was broken when Chip was recognized and the news spread through the crowd like wildfire. In a matter of seconds one continuous roar rolled from the stands.

Beldon hurried to the chief umpire, "Hooks" Bolton, spoke briefly to the surprised man, and then motioned to

ONE PITCH!

Pat Reynolds, the Salem coach. Rockwell extended a hand to Chip and joined the little group at the plate. Then, as though by peremptory command, that great throng quieted. Every person in the park was watching Beldon, the umpire, Pat Reynolds, and Henry Rockwell.

Beldon was doing the talking, reviewing the chase and the capture. Then he drew the fake contract from his pocket and handed it to Rockwell. Reynolds and the umpire crowded close to the Valley Falls mentor and craned their necks as he examined the fateful document.

The crowd in the stands must have sensed that this was the contract they'd read about because the stillness was broken by a giant explosion. It grew in such range and volume that a person couldn't hear the sound of his own voice even if he was shouting with all his might. Chip's teammates gathered in a tight knot behind the mound and waited and hoped that this huddle meant Chip had been given a green light.

"So," Beldon concluded, "Hilton is in the clear! And he's eligible to play, Rock, if and when you want to use him."

Rockwell's glance shot toward the scoreboard, and the veins in his temples bulged under the strain of his concentration upon the decision. Then he shook his head. "No," he said bitterly, at last, "it wouldn't be fair. Chip Hilton has been humiliated and branded and tortured beyond belief for something he knew nothing about. No, it would be the greatest travesty on fair play in the history of baseball!"

"But why?" Beldon cried. "Why? He's eligible! He wants to play! And you certainly need him."

"Not that badly!" Rockwell retorted. "Not badly enough to saddle him with the responsibility of losing a state championship with one pitch! He would carry that memory as long as he lived! Nope, I'd rather lose ten championships!"

"But, Rock," Beldon pleaded, "more than the championship is at stake now. You know how some people are! If Chip doesn't get into this game, there will always be someone who will point to that fact and say he must have been guilty of something! This will clear him completely!"

"Beldon's got something there, Rock," Reynolds said thoughtfully. "Why don't you let Hilton decide? You'll probably hurt him more by keeping him out of the game than by putting him in. Kids are funny that way, you know. They want to win, of course, but if they have to lose they like to lose as a team—to go down together!"

Rockwell turned abruptly away and headed straight for Chip. The crowd's noise died away as the fans followed his progress. Reaching Chip's side, Rockwell draped an arm around his shoulders and shook him gently. "This is a tough spot, Chipper," he said softly, "and it's up to you to make the decision. Last inning, score tied, bases loaded, two down, and the count at three and two—"

Chip didn't even realize what Rockwell was trying to say. He had been lacing his spikes, hurrying to get ready. Then, as the discussion at the plate had continued, he began to fear that Reynolds didn't want him to play.

"You mean it's all right with Salem if I play? Then I'm ready!"

Chip tore off his sports coat, stripped the tie from his collar, and popped the buttons pulling off his white dress shirt as Paddy Jackson handed him a VF jersey. "Some uniform!" he said, smiling at Rockwell.

"The uniform doesn't make the ballplayer!" Stewart said dryly.

The grim lines on Rockwell's face relaxed, and for a long moment he stood there trying to control the sudden surge of emotion gripping his whole being. He didn't dare trust his voice until he forced himself to turn away and read the ominous figures on the scoreboard once more. That did it, and he'd regained his composure when he pivoted back to Stewart.

"Give the umpire and the scorekeeper the lineup change, Chet. Chip's in for Lefty Peters, hitting seventh, behind Trullo. Carey goes to right field and Smith behind the plate.

"Now, Chip, the hitter is Hartman—left fielder—batting in the third spot. Likes 'em fast! Fouled off two of Soapy's fake curve balls. If you feel right after your warm-up, you might try something soft. But that's up to you and Soapy. Remember, the count's three and two, and everything depends on one pitch. The game either ends with that one pitch—and with it the loss of the championship—or it's a new ball game!"

Chet Stewart came bustling back in time to speak out of turn and to surprise Chip and Rockwell by lapsing entirely out of character. "And if we go into extra innings, Chip, Rock'll let you put on the rest of your uniform!"

They smiled and the tension was broken. Rockwell waved toward the umpire and pointed to Chip. The crowd, concentrating on the scene in front of the Valley Falls dugout, caught the gesture, realized its significance, and again the din was deafening.

Chip walked swiftly out to the mound, and each step brought an increase in the crowd ovation until finally it sounded like a sonic boom.

Every Big Red on the field met Chip at the mound, crowding around, pounding him on the back and the shoulders and the head and just anywhere to let him know how they felt. Chip needed a drink of water then, bad. But he felt an even bigger lump in his throat, if that was possible, a second later when Rick Parcels came trotting over from third base.

Parcels grabbed Chip's hand and pumped his arm, smiling, and added his good wishes. "I'm sure glad it wasn't true, Chip. Guess everyone's glad from the sound of the cheers. It's a good thing for us you didn't start! Good luck!"

Chip toed the slab, and began taking his eight warmup throws. As he burned them in to Soapy, he realized, for the first time, how strange he must look. But the importance of that one pitch came flooding back. *One pitch!* Now he knew how Soapy must have felt. Guess the best pitcher in the world wouldn't want to make this throw . . . Well . . . why make it? . . . Because there wasn't any other way—

Wait a minute . . . There was a way. . . .

On the last warm-up pitch, Soapy pegged the ball down to second and joined Chip in front of the mound. As the umpire called, "Hilton now pitching for Smith," Chip told Soapy what he planned to do.

"But it's risky, Chip. Skip it! It's too risky!"

Chip's hand closed over Soapy's wrist. "Of course it's risky," he whispered. "That's the reason it will work. They'll never expect it! You call it!"

"But why don't we tell Cody now?"

"Because they'll see us and catch on! Now—"

"But what if Cody misses the sign?"

"Cody won't miss it! You just call it!"

Soapy trudged back to the plate, adjusted his mask, squatted, and gave the sign. Chip nodded, toed the rubber, and took his stretch. Then he lowered his hands and counted, "One-one thousand, no! Two-two thousand and throw!"

Chip's next action was so fast and so unexpected that only two people saw the play coming. Rockwell saw it coming because he caught Collins's return sign to Soapy. But his "No! No!" was too late.

Pat Reynolds saw Aikin's big lead off second, but his warning "Back! Back!" was never heard.

But every fan saw the play, saw the pivot and the throw to Cody Collins, who dove for the bag and the ball and blocked Aikin a foot from the base for the final out of that hectic seventh inning!

CHAPTER 20

Pitchers' Duel

THE PICK-OFF PLAY had surprised most of the Big Reds as much as it had surprised Aikin. The tension of that action-packed inning had drawn each Big Reds' nerves as tight as the strings of a piano, and the release sent them racing for the dugout, each yelling at the top of his voice.

Chip grabbed Cody's hand and nearly pulled the little fighter off his feet. "Atta boy, Cody," he cried, "I knew you'd get Soapy's sign! What'd I tell you, Soapy? You see that stop?"

Soapy pursed his lips and shook his head. "Not me, Chip! I didn't see it! I just gave the sign and closed my eyes!"

Rockwell was as excited as anyone else. He hugged Chip, and as he did so, the fans gave them both a tremendous ovation. Chip waved his hand and ducked down into the dugout where Stewart was holding his game pants. "Guess you can put these on now!" Stewart exclaimed jubilantly. "What a play! What a play!"

PITCHERS' DUEL

Rick Parcels should've been tired and disheartened. He'd pitched seven long innings, and his teammates had given him a comfortable lead right up to the top of that memorable seventh. But he didn't show it. In fact, he seemed stronger than ever. If his spirits had been affected by the Big Reds' rally, he gave no evidence of it.

Chip was hustling into his pants in a corner of the dugout, shielded by Chet Stewart and Pop Brown, and he was hoping that the Big Reds would have a big inning. He wanted to get in a few warm-up throws before he went back on the mound, but Parcels had different ideas. He set the Big Reds down one-two-three. Schwartz hit one right back to the box; Cohen went for one across his wrists, driving a slow roller to Burns, Salem's second sacker; and Badger topped a two-bounce grass cutter to Aikin. All three were easy outs. So Chip wasn't able to get in any extra warm-up throws and had to walk out to the mound for the bottom of the eighth to face Hartman, who'd been left at the plate on the pick-off play.

Salem's outfield was rated the best in the state for several reasons. Hartman, Shea, and Erickson, batting in that order in the third, fourth, and fifth spots, were fast, good fielders with strong throwing arms, and they all hit the long ball. In addition, they were all lefties, triple trouble for a righty hurler.

Chip knew all about this trio; he knew they'd broken up a lot of ball games. It was important to get a good start with the first one of them.

Hartman had all the marks of a power hitter. The tall left fielder held his bat high, elbows away from his body, and assumed a wide, solid stance. Chip remembered the two other games he'd pitched to Hartman during the regular season. He remembered that Hartman had nicked him for two solid singles, both from his fastball. So he bent a darting hook around Hartman's waist for a called strike and then teased him with a high outside fireball. Hartman looked it over, and that evened the count.

Chip came back with another curve and Hartman took a full swing, getting a piece of it, the ball clearing Smith's head and bouncing up against the grandstand for the one-and-two count.

Chip was ahead now, and he shook Soapy off until he got the sign for the slider. He aimed for the center of the plate and released the ball with a high overhand delivery, swung through with his body, finishing a bit out of position but sending the darting ball past Hartman's full swing for the strikeout.

Soapy powered the ball to Biggie and the horsehide flew around the horn to Cody, Speed, Chris, and back to Cohen. Biggie tossed the ball to Chip, and Shea was up.

Shea was the big gun of the big three, a fixture in the cleanup spot, and he looked the part. The powerful center fielder was built like Cohen but on a slightly smaller scale. He walked up to the plate swinging three bats, cocky and determined. His teammates and the Salem fans gave him a great hand and then got on Chip, yelling and jeering.

"Here goes your ball game, Hilton!"

"Can I have your autograph? Kiss that ball good-bye!"

"Better walk him! Better put him on!"

Chip wasn't walking anyone, wasn't going to put the winning run on base if he could help it. He waited behind the mound, perfectly relaxed, until Shea tossed the two extra bats away and stepped confidently into the batter's box. Shea tapped the plate, lifted his bat in a high overhead stretch, assumed his stance, and glowered at Chip, arrogance expressed in his every move.

Chip took Soapy's sign and then toed the rubber. Shea had challenged him, and Chip was determined to throw his best at the bulky hitter. Working swiftly, he poured his fast one inside, just high enough and close enough to drive Shea back from the plate for ball one; he caught the outside corner with his slider to even the count; and he went ahead with a darting curve around the knees. Next, Chip drove a blinding fastball high outside for ball two and then looped the blooper right smack across the center of the plate. Shea didn't even swing; he was still posing his war club on his shoulder when the umpire called him out.

Erickson was lean and wiry, and he snapped his wrists through beautifully. Chip wasn't sure, but he figured Erickson might be fooled with curves, might at least be induced to hit them in the dirt. But Chip didn't curve his first pitch. He took a chance that Erickson might take one, might want to get a look at him, so he drilled his fast one right in the center of the strike zone.

Erickson watched it go by and stepped out of the box to dust his hands. Right then Chip made up his mind that Erickson had seen the last fastball Chip Hilton was going to serve up to him that day. Chip used his darting hook next and then a teasing change-up that the skinny right fielder topped to send a high bouncing ground ball straight at Cody for an easy out at first. That ended the inning.

That's the way the game went, right through the bottom of the thirteenth. Parcels and Chip, matching one another in a tense pitchers' duel, continued setting the hitters down in order. The fans had quieted now, tired out by the earlier excitement and the long game, sitting on their hands for the most part, and wondering how long it would be until one of these high school phenoms would break.

The radio and television commentators had been thrilled by the action in the earlier innings and had been given plenty to describe. Now they were having a hard time finding something to talk about and became worried their audiences would be bored by the long struggle. They didn't have to worry about the fans in Salem and Valley Falls however. In those two towns, only one program interested the fans, and they meant to sit right by their radios or TVs until the game was over.

Adams and Weaver had no particular love for Salem, but they were two of the most rabid supporters the Sailors had for this game. After checking out of the motel, Adams had parked nearby on a side street and eagerly turned on the radio:

> *It was a tough spot, possibly the toughest situation any high school pitcher ever faced, but Hilton had ice water in his veins, proving to everyone who saw the play that he pitches with more than his arm. He came through the fire with one of the greatest clutch pick-off plays this observer has ever seen. And now it's a new ball game, with the score all tied up at 9-9—and Valley Falls—*

Adams nearly tore the radio button from the dash as he turned it off. "That jerk!" he exploded. "That lousy show-off!"

Weaver was more worried than angry. He was worried about the bets he and Adams had placed, but he was also worried about Delson. "You think he'll sell us out?" he asked abruptly.

Adams's head jerked around as though pulled by a string. His close-set eyes were mean and angry, and the veins on the side of his neck were thickly corded. "You mean Delson? He don't know nothin'!" He gestured contemptuously. "He's the one that pulled everythin'! He got the signature and showed the contract to the sports scribbler! No one's got anything on us!"

PITCHERS' DUEL

"What d'ya think they'll do to him? What can they do?"

Adams reached for the radio knob again. "Nothin'!" he said shortly. "Nothin' at all!"

And now it's Salem's turn at bat, with the big end of the stick coming up—Hartman, Shea, and Erickson—

Adams again turned the knob. "I can't stand this!" he said irritably. "I'm goin' over there on the grass and do some thinkin'. Let me know when it's over."

University had been thronged by hundreds of Valley Falls faithfuls that morning. A few had come up with the team earlier in the week, and some had arrived Friday night, but the bulk of the Big Reds' fans had driven over that morning. No matter when they had arrived, all of them had managed to get the paper carrying the story of Chip's ineligibility.

Petey Jackson had been one of the first to hear the story, and he rushed to tell John Schroeder. Schroeder had gone into a huddle with Doc Jones and worked up a plan to keep the story from reaching Mary Hilton until they'd gotten her to the university and all the facts were known.

That explained why Mary Hilton, John Schroeder, and Doc Jones took off on the two-hour drive to the university that afternoon. Mary Hilton was concerned about the time. "We'll be a little late, won't we?" she asked.

Doc Jones assured her that championship games were always long-drawn-out affairs, and if they arrived at the game in the late afternoon, they'd probably be in time to see the most interesting part. He also said it was too bad that the radio in John Schroeder's car wasn't working, but they could listen to CDs if she wanted.

PITCHERS' DUEL

Schroeder went along with Doc on that, laughing it off, but then, of course, he didn't know that Jones had actually pulled out a whole fistful of wires.

Mary Hilton had always known John Schroeder was a careful driver, but this was ridiculous! Ten miles an hour below the speed limit was being a little too careful. For a man on the way to a ball game, she thought, he made an awful lot of stops, really for no reason at all except to find out the score.

Doc always made it a point personally to dash into the gas station or convenience store to get the score. He may not have been a very accurate reporter, but it was for a good cause. "The kids are way out in front!" he assured his listeners, blandly omitting to tell them that it was the Salem kids.

They stopped for the last time just outside University. Something happened at the last stop that Mary Hilton didn't understand. Doc Jones came flying back, puffing and wheezing and as excited as she'd ever seen anyone in her life.

"It's a tie game!" he shouted. "Nine to nine! Last of the eighteenth! And Chip's pitching! Step on it!"

Mary Hilton was further bewildered when John Schroeder snatched his Valley Falls baseball cap off his head, tossed it over his shoulder into the back seat, and yelled, "Yippee!"

Before Mary had figured that out, they were at University Field, and Schroeder and Jones each had her by a hand and were running for the gate.

Chip had never felt better in his life. He had plenty of smoke, and his curve and his slider were darting streaks of lightning. In spite of the wind that had sprung up and was blowing briskly into his face, his control was perfect. So far, he had thirteen strikeouts to his credit.

PITCHERS' DUEL

There were two down and Erickson was at bat when Schroeder and Jones arrived, fairly dragging Mary Hilton between them. Some of the grandstand fans had gone home, and there were several vacant seats directly behind home plate. Doc spotted them and led the way, snatching up a paper lying on an end seat and handing it to Mary. "Spread that on the bench," he said excitedly. "Keep your suit clean!" He grabbed Schroeder by the arm. "Wow! What a game this must have been! Eighteen innings!"

Mary Hilton was still holding the paper when Chip wound up and pulled the string on his curve, and he had his fourteenth strikeout. The fans gave him a big hand as he walked to the dugout. Chip lifted his cap and then walked to the bat rack and got his favorite wooden bat. He was on deck behind Trullo.

Parcels was emotionally and physically drained. He'd gone eighteen long, nerve-racking innings, and, unfortunately, he wasn't blessed with the frame and the stamina that Chip possessed. Besides, the wind was affecting his control.

Rockwell had noted Parcels's fatigue, and he told Trullo, "Look 'em over, Nick! He's dead tired. Wait him out!"

Trullo waited him out, and it paid off. Nick worked Parcels for the full count and then walked when Rick barely missed the outside corner. Chip was up. So far, batting left-handed, he had singled in the eighth, flied out in the eleventh, grounded out in the fourteenth, and slashed a two-bagger against the right-field fence in the sixteenth. Now he was in the top of the nineteenth, batting five hundred, with a chance to win his own game. That is, if he didn't have to advance Nick.

Rockwell had been waiting for a break, but now that they had it, he wasn't sure what to do. Chip was a good hitter, and Parcels had handcuffed Carey, who followed Chip, the whole game. Also, since Soapy's seventh-inning round-tripper, Rick had struck out the redhead three times.

Chip, on the first-base side of the plate, went through his batting ritual. Just before he stepped into the batter's box, he glanced at Chet Stewart in the third-base coaching box, but Chet was looking out at the scoreboard. Chip was on his own! He dug in, noted the positions of the outfielders, and took a good toehold. At that moment Hooks Bolton, the plate umpire, called time.

Pat Reynolds walked out to the mound to talk to Parcels, and Chip stepped away from the plate. He knew what that conference was all about. Reynolds was instructing Rick to put him on, to give him an intentional walk. The Salem coach was matching wits with Rockwell!

Chip was right. Parcels threw four straight balls nowhere near the plate, and Chip trotted down to first, Trullo moving to second.

Carey followed orders and tried to lay it down, but Parcels kept the ball at the top of the strike zone. Carl popped up to the catcher for the first out. Soapy came up then, grim-faced and determined, but as tight as a drum. His swing was just as tight. With the count at one and one, Rockwell, desperate and taking a long chance, put on the hit and run. Soapy tried too hard, however, missing the ball by a foot.

Trullo and Chip were away with Rick's pitch, but Nick wasn't fast enough. Overton's peg cut him down at third by ten feet. Chip overran second purposely, hoping to draw a throw, but Curry was too smart and held the ball. That made it two away; the count on Soapy, one ball and two strikes. After a close one evened the count at two-two, Parcels broke Soapy's heart with a slow curve for strike three, and the Big Reds' big chance was gone.

Chip warmed up quickly and eyed the hitter moving to the plate. It was Curry, Salem's third baseman, and Chip breathed easier. He had Curry's number: the number three—three strikes.

Kimmel, Salem's tall first baseman, was the fourth Sailor who hit left-handed. Chip had his number, too, but this time Kimmel was late on his swing and got a piece of the ball, lifting a high fly behind third. Badger went back for it, but Trullo, playing toward center field, cut over for the catch. Chris called, "Take it, Nick! It's all yours!"

Trullo was coming in at full speed, hustling to get under the ball. It was this hustle that caused the trouble. He got there too soon. Poised for the catch, he brought a gasp of heartbreaking dismay from his teammates and every Valley Falls fan in the park when he suddenly backtracked and missed the catch. The wind had caught the spinning ball and driven it back over his head.

Kimmel was playing heads-up baseball, running everything out, and he reached third just before a frantic Chris Badger recovered the ball and burned it in to Chip, covering the bag.

Baseball victories often depend upon unpredictable events. These are called the breaks of the game. This was one of those breaks—and it went against the Big Reds.

As soon as the ball was in Chip's hands, Rockwell called time. This break could mean the loss of the game. One bad play now, one little bobble, and this game would be over. "Tough break, Chip," he said warmly. "It's just one of those things. Don't let it get you down! Stay in there! You can pull it out!" Rockwell was stalling for time, giving the kids a chance to settle down.

PITCHERS' DUEL

Chip waved with understanding to Trullo, who was shaking his head and slowly walking back to his position. Then Chip nodded grimly and answered Rockwell. "I'm all right, Coach," he said sturdily.

Reynolds called for the squeeze then, but Chip spoiled that by keeping the ball first high and then low. Overton fouled off two twisters before striking out on a fireball that nearly knocked Soapy off his feet. That made it two down, with the winning run on third and Parcels at bat. Chip half expected Coach Reynolds to send in a pinch hitter then, but it was Rick himself who stepped into the batter's box.

Chip cross-fired a fastball for a called strike, pulled the string on a slow twister that just missed the low outside corner, and got ahead on a slider that cut under Rick's bat for strike two. Then Chip missed the outside corner with two more curves and it was three and two, the full count.

Once again the game hinged on one pitch. Chip took his time and then put everything he had on his fast one. Parcels swung wildly, barely topping the ball and sending it spinning just outside the limed third-base line. At the crack of the bat, Kimmel broke for home and Parcels sprinted to first.

Chip dashed for the ball but Badger beat him to it, stabbing desperately at the spinning sphere with his glove hand, trying to knock it away from the line. Just before his last frantic stab, however, the ball struck a small pebble; bobbed crazily into fair territory, too late for a play at the plate or at first; and spun slowly to a stop while Badger, Soapy, and Chip stood helplessly watching. The game was over!

The Sailors were the new baseball champions of the state!

CHAPTER 21

The Last Straw

THE SALEM locker room was a frenzy of emotional release. The Sailors were releasing all of their pent-up hopes and fears in one jubilant cheer after another. They quieted to listen to Rockwell's congratulations and to give a cheer for Valley Falls, and then they were at it all over again.

In the Valley Falls locker room the contrast was almost unbelievable. The room was quiet, almost silent. One or two of the players had taken their showers, and the faint hiss of the spraying water was the only sound that could be heard. The other players were sitting in front of their lockers thinking or slowly removing their uniforms. Right after the game, Rockwell had given them a little talk, blaming himself, as usual, for the defeat.

"It's all right, kids," he had said consolingly, "you were great! I pulled the boneheads. Let's forget about it! You can't win all the time! Someone has to lose! And since it had to be us, let's be good sports about it and take it with our heads and our chins up! OK?

"Right now, I want to congratulate each of you for your part in playing on the best baseball team I ever coached! I'm proud to have been your coach."

Rockwell then had shaken hands with each player, finishing up with the seniors last, warmly gripping the hands of Soapy, Biggie, Speed, Red, and, at the end, Rock's large hand folded over Chip's. Everyone stood silently, and each senior felt as if the Rock had been saying something personal just to him. The room was so quiet that the soft sound of the water in the shower room seemed like a roaring torrent.

After Rockwell left, Chip leaned back against the door of his locker. Beside him, Nick Trullo was bent forward, elbows on knees, head supported by his hands. Nick blamed himself for losing the game. Chip didn't look, but he knew Nick wasn't sitting that way because of fatigue. The big southpaw was trying to conceal his tear-welled eyes. Chip felt awkward and uncomfortable and wondered what he could say to help his heartbroken friend. He was glad when Rick Parcels came in and walked directly to his side.

"Tough luck, Chip," Parcels said, extending his hand and helping Chip to his feet. "It was a bad break."

"The best team won, Rick," Chip said warmly. "You pitched a great game! You had to go the whole way too. Nice going!"

A few minutes later, Beldon, Reynolds, and Rockwell came in together. They were talking about the game, and every player in the room overheard their conversation.

"It was a tough break, Rock," Reynolds was saying in his soft drawl. "Particularly in view of all the trouble."

THE LAST STRAW

"It sure was!" Beldon added. "By the way, Rock, while I have you two coaches together, maybe we ought to discuss the protest."

Rockwell interrupted him. "We have no protest!" he said quickly. "We lost fair and square! If we'd been able to pitch Chip all the way, it might've been a different story or it might not. That's what makes baseball such a great game—the uncertainty of everything! We lost to a better team. No, I'll take that back, we lost to a great team! The Big Reds and I have nothing but admiration for the new champions of the state! But watch out next year!"

Mary Hilton was still clutching the newspaper when the game ended. The first thing she'd seen was Turk's story about Chip. During the last inning, while her excited companions concentrated on the play on the field, she read the story about the contract. Throughout that disastrous nineteenth inning, she sat quietly thinking about the long series of difficulties her son had faced all through the season. She knew that somehow the truth had been discovered in time for Chip to play, but she was amazed that his spirit had not been broken completely. Her pride in her tall son brought the mist into her eyes.

Later, after that fatal last play, she assured John Schroeder and Doc Jones that she'd prefer to go right home. When Schroeder suggested they take Chip along, she shook her head. "No," she said firmly, "Chip belongs with his teammates."

The ride home and the long wait until Chip finally arrived seemed an eternity to his mom. It was nearly midnight when she heard his steps on the porch. An instant later Chip's arms were around her, and he was swinging her around and around, laughing and laughing. But he wasn't fooling his mom a bit.

Mary Hilton knew her son, knew when he was tired, disappointed, and low in spirits. She knew he was worried now about the story of his ineligibility, so she beat him to the punch, making it easy for him. "I saw the game, Chip," she said, laughing at his surprise. "And," she continued, "I read the story in the paper! I'm proud of you, Chip. Proud that you controlled yourself."

That was the opening Chip needed. He poured out the story, relieved he could get it off his chest. He told her about Adams and Weaver and the capture of Delson. As Mary Hilton learned more of the details, she began to understand why John Schroeder and Doc Jones had been so insistent that she go along to the game. But she didn't tell Chip about that; she just tried to comfort him.

"After all, it was just a game, Chip," she said, "one of many you've been through and only one of many more you'll go through when you go to college. You can't expect to win all the time. The other team likes to win a championship, too, once in a while."

"I know that, Mom. It isn't so much the loss of the championship. Salem's got a great team, and it wasn't a disgrace to lose to a team like that. It's the Rock! And his job!"

"I wouldn't worry about that too much, Chip. After all, Coach Rockwell has been here too many years for anything like that to happen. Everyone in town likes him. I wish I could tell you what they've got planned for him Monday night at the banquet, but it's all supposed to be a surprise. He could be the principal if he wanted the job."

"But he doesn't want to be the principal, Mom. He just wants to be the coach! Remember what I heard Doc Jones say? Remember what he said? That if we lost, the mayor was going to announce Rock's retirement?"

THE LAST STRAW

"Yes, I remember, Chip. But I wouldn't put too much in it. You may be sure J. P. Ohlsen will have something to say about that! Sleep in tomorrow morning. We'll have a late breakfast."

But Chip couldn't sleep that night. He tossed and turned, and all night he fought the thoughts and worries interrupting his rest. In the morning, he tiptoed down the stairs and out on the porch. Sitting there on the steps next to Hoops, he anxiously checked through the front and sports pages of the *Post* and the *Times*. There was nothing about Rockwell's retirement. He breathed a sigh of relief and began reading the story about the game.

Pete Williams's story played up the breaks of the game and lauded Chip's pitching. He called Soapy an unsung hero and pronounced the season a great success. Chip was most interested in Williams's reference to the fake contract:

> Except for the regrettable, but understandable, action of the state eligibility committee, the championship might have been retained. The one bright spot in the report of the false ineligibility charge was the complete vindication of William "Chip" Hilton. It is understood that one of the perpetrators of the serious hoax is under arrest and that the police are seeking several others, two of whom are reported to be local residents.

Muddy Waters was, if nothing else, consistent. He continued his attacks on Rockwell. He maintained that the Big Reds mentor should have pitched Trullo in the first game so he could have been available for the championship game. He cited the previous year's victory and

PITCHERS' DUEL

Trullo's great pitching. The part that really angered Chip, however, was Waters's unfair reference to Rockwell's responsibility for the eligibility difficulty:

> Rockwell is directly responsible for the loss of the state championship. A coach's first responsibility is the team under his supervision. The parents of the players expect the responsible person to behave responsibly. Henry Rockwell failed to protect his team members from contact with the person or persons responsible for the incident that resulted in William Hilton's suspension until the last of the seventh inning. This glaring failure is but one more reflection upon the veteran coach's methods and an additional recommendation for his retirement.

Chip crumpled the paper in his hands. This article would just add fuel to the fire. He wished he could think of something to do.

That night Chip and his mom had a long talk. Chip's graduation from high school had been an important goal for each of them—for Chip, because it brought him closer to the day when he could be the head of their home, assume its responsibilities, and help his mom; for Mrs. Hilton, because it was a big step toward her dream of a college education for her son.

"I'm proud of you, Chip," she said softly, "proud of your success in sports and your achievements in school. It doesn't seem so awfully long ago when you were just a little guy, and your dad and I were dreaming of the day you'd graduate from high school."

Chip hugged his mother and then dropped his head to her shoulder. There was no teasing and laughing and swinging around tonight. This moment was a communion that comes all too seldom to mother and son. Mary Hilton held Chip tightly, gripped by that bittersweetness that comes to every mother when she realizes her son is growing up. Chip, on the other hand, lost himself in the refuge every boy treasures most, the haven of peace he finds in his mother's arms.

Graduation day dawned bright and sunny, and nine o'clock found Chip and his classmates, nervous and excited, in the auditorium for graduation rehearsal. It was eleven o'clock before Zimmerman was satisfied and dismissed them with strict instructions to assemble in the main gym at 1:30-sharp!

Taps Browning was waiting on the broad landing outside the main entrance when the rowdy seniors spilled out the wide doors. He rushed anxiously toward Chip's side and handed him a copy of the *Times*.

"Look at the front page, Chip," he said breathlessly. "Rockwell's been retired!"

Chip's heart sank. Biggie, Soapy, Speed, and Red crowded around him as he unfolded the paper. There it was, just as he'd feared.

Coach Henry Rockwell Retired
Mentor Past Retirement Age
Ruling Effective July 1

In the absence of J. P. Ohlsen, chairman of the Valley Falls Board of Education, Mayor Condon announced this morning that Henry Rockwell, a member of the physical education staff and the coach of the Big Reds football, basketball, and baseball teams for the past thirty-seven years, would be retiring as of July 1.

Rockwell is two years past the retirement age

established by the state department of education, and his tenure of service qualifies him for full pension benefits.

Under Rockwell's direction, the local high school athletic teams achieved considerable success. However, the application of the state retirement act makes it imperative that he be replaced.

No mention of a successor was made in the brief announcement, and since the notification was received shortly before this paper went to press, it was impossible to contact Rockwell and secure information about his future plans.

"I knew it!" Chip murmured. "I knew it!"

"The Rock didn't," Speed said bitterly. "You can bet on that!"

"Wonder where he is?" Soapy mused.

"Chet wasn't here either," Biggie said thoughtfully. "Bet they're in the office."

"Well, let's go see," Chip suggested.

Rockwell wasn't in the office. They couldn't find Chet Stewart anywhere in the building either. The boys walked out to the broad landing of the gym entrance and sat down on the steps, each player trying to figure out what to do.

"Bet they're at Rock's house!" Soapy said suddenly. "What d'ya say?"

"I say we go!" Chip said grimly. "But I think we ought to take the present we got him with us. Come on, it's in my locker."

"That's a good idea," Biggie agreed. "It'll give us a chance to talk to him."

Red said thoughtfully, "I guess Rock could use a little moral support right now."

"That's what's wrong with this picture," Speed muttered. "How come Ohlsen and Stanton and Thomas let the mayor and his crowd get away with it?"

"Ohlsen didn't know about it," Chip said abruptly. "He was out of town! He's coming back just for the banquet tonight!"

"Well, how about Stanton and Thomas?" Schwartz asked.

"They were outnumbered," Chip explained. "You see, the mayor had Davis, Greer, and Cantwell all lined up against Rockwell. Then when Ohlsen was called out of town on business, why—" Chip stopped, but it was too late.

"Hey," Soapy said sharply, "you've been holdin' out on us! You know stuff! Come on! Give!"

Chip had no recourse then, so he told his buddies everything, except that losing the championship game had worked against Rockwell. It was a somber group who stood on the Rockwell porch a few minutes later. Chip was clutching the little package and trying desperately to figure out what he was going to say, but his mind wouldn't function. He was lost.

Soapy had been right. Rockwell was at home, and Chet Stewart and a stranger were with him. But Mrs. Rockwell smiled graciously as she ushered the five boys into the living room. "Here's some more visitors, Hank," she said. "Suppose you introduce your guest."

Rockwell gestured toward the boys. "This is a coincidence. Dave," he said, "here are the very guys we were talking about. Boys, this is Dave Young. He's here to talk tonight at the banquet. Mr. Young is the director of athletics at State, and since you're all going to be up there this fall, he's a good man to know. Dave, this is Soapy Smith, Biggie Cohen, Red Schwartz, Speed Morris, and Chip Hilton. Chip was the captain of the ball club."

The boys shook hands with Young and then stood awkwardly shifting from one foot to the other.

Chip broke the silence. "I . . . we wanted to see you, Coach, before graduation and before the banquet tonight to . . . to give you a little present from just the five of us—"

Soapy tried to help out. "You see, Coach, we're all seniors, and we won't be playing for Valley Falls anymore and—"

Rockwell laughed. "I know exactly how you feel," he said. "It looks as though we're all in the same boat." He nodded toward the paper on the table. "I guess you've seen the *Times*. You see, Soapy, I won't be coaching Valley Falls anymore either. I'm guess I'll be graduating too!"

A few minutes later the five friends were on their way to the Sugar Bowl. They were silent for a while, each feeling that the little expedition somehow hadn't measured up to their anticipation.

"Speed's right," Cohen said slowly. "Something's wrong!"

"Yeah," Schwartz agreed, "something sure is wrong."

"Maybe he's gonna run for mayor!" Soapy suggested.

"That's silly!" Schwartz said in disgust. "The Rock doesn't want to do anything except coach! Don't be a dork!"

Cohen summed up everybody's thoughts. "It's a dirty deal," he said glumly, "but you know the Rock! He's tough! He wouldn't let anyone know how he feels!"

It was nearly one o'clock before they reached the Sugar Bowl and by that time the news was on the lips of everyone in town. The story caused almost as much confusion as the senior administration day. Most residents were resentful and openly critical. Practically everyone, with the exception of a small group headed by Jerry Davis, was sorry to learn the bad news.

THE LAST STRAW

At one o'clock the *Post* came out with an early edition. It should have been called the "Rockwell Special." Practically the entire front page and all the sports pages were devoted to the retirement story and to Rockwell's achievements. His thirty-seven-year record in every sport was shown in one column, and the list of Big Reds championships won under his direction down through the years was listed in another. Smack in the middle of the page was his picture. Chip felt a glow of happiness as he read the double-column story. At least the *Post* was standing by the Rock.

Coach Henry Rockwell to Retire
Veteran Mentor's Last Year
Announcement Made Today

The Valley Falls Board of Education announced today that Coach Henry Rockwell would retire from his duties at Valley Falls High School on July 1. The veteran strategist is completing his thirty-seventh year of service.

During the thirty-seven years Coach Rockwell has been at the helm of the Valley Falls athletic program, the Big Reds have dominated the southern part of the state in football, basketball, and baseball. Rockwell's teams have won twenty-two of thirty-seven section championships in football, nineteen in basketball, and fourteen in baseball. In All-State competition, the Big Reds forces have won more titles than any other school.

Rockwell's success has not been limited to victories, championships, and titles. His personal interest, unswerving confidence, and loyalty to each young athlete who has played for him has built up in this community a love and respect that is a far greater tribute to the man than the hundreds of cups, trophies, medals, and plaques on display in the Big Reds' trophy room.

There was much more to the story, but by this time Soapy had consumed his third cheeseburger, second order of onion rings, and a large hot fudge sundae. He was ready for action. "Let's go!" he said. "Let's do something!"

"What?" Speed queried. "Just do what?"

Soapy had twenty answers for that question. They wouldn't show up for graduation. They'd skip the banquet. They'd picket Mayor Condon's office. They'd get up a petition. They'd burn Condon in effigy. They'd burn the whole board of education in effigy—that is, everybody except Ohlsen, Stanton, and Thomas. They'd . . . Well, wasn't that enough?

While that tirade was pouring from Soapy's lips, Chip had been trying to figure out some course of action, but nothing seemed to make sense. He finally decided that the best thing was to go see the most powerful man in town. "Tomorrow," he announced decisively, "we'll go see J. P. Ohlsen and find out if he can't do something about this! Right now, we'd better get moving or we'll be late for graduation."

"Who cares?" Soapy demanded. "Graduation ain't gonna be no fun, now—nor the banquet, neither!" he concluded glumly.

An hour later the Valley Falls High School graduating class was seated on the stage in the auditorium. Chip felt kind of foolish sitting there with people looking at him and his classmates as if they were on display in a store window. Yet a moment later he located his mom in the audience of proud relatives and, as far away as she was, he could see the pride shining in her eyes. Suddenly he was filled with such warmth of gratitude that the weight in his chest almost choked off his breath.

Chip didn't hear much of the graduation addresses because he was thinking back through the four short years he'd been in Valley Falls High School. He imagined he felt almost like a guy must feel when he loses all his friends. He looked at his mom again and resolved he'd get through college if it was the last thing he ever did. He'd come out with a real education, equipped to do something worthwhile, something meaningful . . .

Four years wasn't so long. If he worked hard, those years would fly just like the past four years. Then he'd be sitting up on another stage, and his mom would be sitting in the audience looking just as beautiful and as proud as she looked today.

Chip saw Mr. and Mrs. Cohen, Mr. and Mrs. Morris, Mr. and Mrs. Smith, and Red Schwartz's father and mother, and he wondered if Biggie, Red, Speed, Soapy, and he would all graduate from college together. Anyway, they had all decided to start out together in September at State.

Just then, the speaker sat down, and there was a great burst of applause. Chip joined in too. He tried to remember what the speaker had said, but all he could recall was something about the warmth students should feel for their teachers and the loyalty they should give to their ideals. Chip looked around for Coach Rockwell, but he wasn't there.

A little later Chip heard Biggie's name and then his own name, and he got up and followed the girl in front of him until he reached Principal Zimmerman and took the long, white cylinder that said forever and forever he was a high school graduate and ready for college!

PITCHERS' DUEL

He was standing in front of his seat when he heard them call "Robert Smith." He watched Soapy walk slowly up to Zimmerman. He half expected Soapy to come out with some kind of a wisecrack—until he saw Soapy's face. His expression was set, determined and intense. Chip saw the redhead looking down to where Mr. and Mrs. Smith sat in the third row, and when Soapy made the turn at the end of the stage and walked back to his seat, he was still looking that way. For the first time Chip realized that everyone took Soapy too much for granted; they didn't really know him.

Chip started thinking about the game and how hard it was to lose. He thought about Rick Parcels and, for the life of him, he couldn't help thinking that Parcels was genuinely glad Chip had gotten out of that hole in the seventh inning. He believed Rick had been glad that everything had been squared up at the top of the eighth so they could fight it out on even terms. Chip was happy that if he had to lose to anyone, it had been to a great guy like Rick.

That foul twister had sure caused a lot of trouble. If only he'd been able to reach that ball when it was outside the line, when it was spinning so crazily around in foul territory. That little twisting ball that had lit foul and then squirmed fair had hurt. It had cost him the game, the Big Reds the tournament, Valley Falls High the championship, and had probably been the last straw that cost the Rock his job.

CHAPTER 22

"We'll Kill 'Em!"

MOST SPORTS dinners are lively and happy occasions, often boisterous in their celebration of a successful season or a championship. However, the great throng of athletes and adults who jammed the banquet hall at the Valley Falls Inn were strangely subdued. Although the appetizer, the entrée, and the dessert were delicious, many people seated at the closely crowded tables merely toyed with their food.

Doc Jones, one of Valley Falls's most popular citizens, was a good toastmaster, with a salty sense of humor. Yet even he quickly sensed the futility of trying to raise the spirits of this crowd. Consequently, he hurried things along, cutting short his announcements and introductions, substituting speed and action for levity. It was a relieved toastmaster who finally arrived at the climax of the evening: the presentation of J. P. Ohlsen who would introduce Henry Rockwell, "Hank" to the older guests of Valley Falls, and "Rock" to every sports-loving enthusiast.

PITCHERS' DUEL

Ohlsen made no effort to speak, but turned and grasped Rockwell's hand and led him to the center of the table where two microphones flanked the state runner-up trophy. The two friends stood with hands clasped, facing the appreciative community, who rose to their feet and cheered. This ovation came from the heart as an expression of love and admiration that could never have been adequately put into words.

When the applause died down a bit, Ohlsen followed Doc Jones's example and made his introduction brief. Raising Rockwell's hand in the air, he said simply, "Our coach!"

Once again cheers and applause rang out from every corner of the room until Ohlsen raised his hands. Then, after a time, the demonstration reluctantly died away, and finally everyone was seated and it was quiet.

Ohlsen waited a moment and then waved his hand dramatically toward the big glass windows that faced Main Street. "You can pull those curtains now," he said.

Everyone turned to look, and there, right on the sidewalk, spotlighted perfectly, was a new red Cadillac. On the hood was a sign that read:

The Henry Rockwell Athletic Center
The House That Rock Built

"Hank, those words will be placed at the top of what used to be known as Ohlsen territory," J. P. announced in a trembling voice. "It was always yours anyway!"

There was another cheer and a storm of applause that was almost deafening. Rockwell stood looking down at the table. Two little muscles stood out on each side of his tightly clamped jaw.

"WE'LL KILL 'EM"

"And, Hank," Ohlsen continued when he could make himself heard again, "here's the title to the car, and this envelope contains all your retirement forms to fill out. A few of us could retire if we had all your money!" Ohlsen regained his composure as he joked, and the audience joined in the laughter.

Rockwell's outstretched hand stopped him. "Excuse me, J. P.," he said softly. "May I say something now?"

Ohlsen nodded. "Why, of course, Hank," he said heartily. "Of course. Go right ahead."

Everyone was looking at Rockwell now, noting his erect carriage, suntanned face, and alert black eyes. Many were thinking that despite his age and years of experience, the Rock seemed right in his prime.

Chip was one of those. He knew the tireless physical energy of his coach, the lightninglike alertness of his mind, and how much he loved his work. "It isn't right," he muttered, "it isn't right."

After a brief pause, Rockwell began to speak. His voice sounded a bit shaky at first, but after a few words, it resonated clear and strong. "I hardly know where to begin, but I suppose I ought to start with the car." He smiled ruefully. "Speed Morris and I have been struggling along with our antiques for a long time. Anyway, it's great, and it's too much. But I appreciate the generosity, and I promise to drive it carefully—if I can get it away from Mrs. Rockwell."

There was a swell of laughter, and when it ceased, Rockwell's face sobered as he continued. "Louise and I have felt, and will always feel, that Valley Falls is our home. We've seen our two sons grow up; go through elementary, middle, and high school here; and then go off to college and to careers in other parts of the country. We know that any success they may have attained or will attain was due to the training and inspiration they received from the people and schools here in Valley Falls. None of us will ever forget the many friendships we have made in this fine town, ones we cherish with all our hearts.

"I will never forget the ups and downs our teams have encountered, the thrills of the successes and the heartaches of the defeats.

"The trophy room and its stories of great deeds fill my heart with pride. But most of all, the friendship of all the fine students who have played for Valley Falls, and for me, is my greatest treasure.

"Now I suppose I must say something about the retirement. I believe a pension means a person is being retired because he has reached an age where there is question about his usefulness in his job. I cannot accept that premise, and I cannot accept the pension.

"So good friends, neighbors, and athletes, for everything else I thank you from the bottom of my heart."

There was no applause, only a silence that was a greater tribute than the cheers had been. Rockwell sat down in his chair between Ohlsen and the guest speaker. The thoughts that ran through the minds of the people in that room carried back through the years. There was sadness in the hearts of most of them, and shame in the hearts of some.

Chip was having a tough time controlling the lump in his throat. Although he succeeded in that effort, he still couldn't keep a tear from rolling down his cheek. His thoughts were flying back through the years he had played for the Rock . . . his broken leg . . . the championships he'd helped to win . . . the championship ball Rock and the team had given him that year he'd had to sit on the bench . . .

"WE'LL KILL 'EM"

Then Chip thought about the pension and looked back at Rockwell. "It's his pride," he muttered. "He's always had pride. Lots of it!"

When Rockwell finished speaking and sat down, the five seniors at the honor table suddenly were aware for the first time what this athletic banquet really meant. This was good-bye. Good-bye to the Big Reds . . . and to Ohlsen Field . . . and to the *Yellow Jacket* . . . and to Prof Rogers and Pop Brown and Principal Zimmerman and Chet Stewart . . . and all their pals. Most of all, good-bye to the Rock.

No more tongue lashings when they were deserved and no more pats on the back when they had them coming. No more private meetings with the Rock in the little athletic office where a guy could speak straight out and say how he felt and be sure his problem, or anything he said, would be welcomed by the man with the friendly black eyes and that crooked smile of understanding.

Chip cleared his throat and shifted in his chair; four other seniors sitting at the graduation table did the same thing. Then, as if from a long way off, they heard J. P. Ohlsen introduce the guest speaker.

D. H. Young, director of athletics at State University, was a regular on the banquet circuit. He was extremely popular with sports fans of the state and was much in demand as an after-dinner speaker. Young considered attendance at these affairs important to his work and accepted as many invitations as possible. He'd welcomed this invitation for several reasons, the most important being his treasured friendship with Henry Rockwell. His speech reflected the warmth and feeling in his heart. Chip didn't hear much of the first part of the speaker's talk, but toward the last he heard every word.

PITCHERS' DUEL

"Statistics show that one in about sixteen hundred students with a high school education achieves something really notable in life. But one out of every seventy-two students with a college education—one out of seventy-two with a college education—leaves his or her mark on the world! Coach Henry Rockwell knows that! He has always valued education. He has always expected his athletes to achieve their best in academics as well as athletics and has never settled for less. It is only appropriate, then, that State University, in conjunction with the Valley Falls Pottery, has established the Coach Henry Rockwell Scholarship at Valley Falls High School, effective next year, to recognize a student demonstrating excellence in academics and athletics, unselfishness in community service, and strength of personal character.

"Additionally, I've learned that a great number of students from this graduating class plan to attend my university in the fall. In particular, five members of the state runner-up baseball team will be with us. As the representative of your university and mine, I am proud to announce the appointment of Coach Henry Rockwell to the coaching staff of State University."

It took several seconds before these giant bombshells exploded the room into the greatest graduation celebration Valley Falls had ever witnessed! The excitement grew and grew until every person was on his feet, cheering and shouting.

Chip didn't remember getting up, but somehow he was on his feet too. As he stood yelling and cheering with the rest of that happy throng, his heart was jumping and his thoughts were racing. This must be a dream . . . Was he hearing things?

"Coach Rockwell has sent us some of our greatest athletes. While he was coaching here at Valley Falls, we were content to let him stay. But now that he's 'retired,' we can take him to State where we've wanted him for the past twenty years!"

It had to be true because everyone else was cheering and applauding. The Rock looked straight at Chip and smiled, nodding his head. It was true!

They'd all be together again—all of them . . . Biggie and Soapy and Red and Speed and . . . and the Rock and him . . . at State!

Then, just as they had clasped hands so many times in tense moments on the football field, on the court, in the dressing room, and before the baseball games during the past four years, and just as if they had rehearsed it a thousand times for this special moment, the five university freshmen around that honor table joined hands. Their eyes shot toward the Rock, and they all had the same thought, which they whispered almost in unison: "We'll kill 'em! We'll kill 'em!"

• • •

CHIP HILTON'S high school days are over! After winning MVP honors in the All-Star Tournament, Chip spends the rest of the summer as an intern with the Parkville Bears, managed by Eddie Duer. When the front running Bears go into an inexplicable tailspin during the last week of their hectic season, Chip, from his position on the dugout bench, thinks he's solved the baffling puzzle of what's happening to Bear pitching and general team morale. But what if he's wrong? How can he be sure without endangering a player and causing irreparable harm for life? Most of the action takes place outside Valley Falls—and there's plenty of it! Even the chance for Chip to be a top draft pick in the First Year Player Draft in Major League Baseball!

Afterword

OCCASIONALLY, I think we all pause to reflect on where we are in our lives and examine how we got there. Sometimes I have to shake myself to realize that I'm the manager of the Cleveland Indians. How did I, who came from a small town in the Texas Panhandle, end up as the manager of a major league baseball team?

The contrast of my childhood years as opposed to my adult years are almost incomparable when it comes to the casual aspects such as location, being around extended family, lifestyles, and travel. However, the concrete aspects are very similar, I'm proud to say.

Few childhood memories, both good and bad, are ever quite as clear and concise at the age of fifty as they were at the age of fifteen. The ones that remain with that same intensity are rare and significant.

One such reflection for me is the fond memory of my childhood role model, Chip Hilton.

I still vividly remember sitting on the floor in my uncle's bedroom between the bookshelf and the bed reading about Chip. I can envision now, as then, Chip scoring the winning basket or making the big play of the game. That same excitement and thrill, the absolute feeling of exhilaration in being successful and competitive, lives within me to this day.

I know without a doubt that it was the Chip Hilton series I read as that young boy on the family farm back in Texas that formed my values on how I wanted to compete in sports, but more importantly, how I wanted to live my life as a man.

I recently reread the book *Strike Three!* and immediately was taken back to that wonderful world of my youth to the point of smelling the fresh cut grass and hearing the pop of the ball as it hit the glove.

What a tremendous gift to have the ability to transport a young man into such a glorious world.

I've said it before and I'll say it again. . . .

Thank you, Clair Bee, for helping mold me in no small way by defining the values of my life today, the exact values I want to pass on to my son.

What an honor for Clair Bee's family to recognize the positive impact he made on so many young men in the fifties and sixties and be willing to take the time to update this amazing series to "fit" today's time and youth.

The new series is a gift I intend to share with my son, praying it will truly be the "guide" it proved to be to me.

I may receive recognition as a manager of a major league baseball team, but more importantly, I want to be recognized as a man who put into practice the values I learned from reading the Chip Hilton series.

MIKE HARGROVE
Manager, Cleveland Indians

more great releases from the

Chip Hilton Sports Series

by Coach Clair Bee

The sports-loving boy, born out of the imagination of Clair Bee, is back! Clair Bee first began writing the Chip Hilton series in 1948. During the next twenty years, over two million copies of the series were sold. Written in the tradition of the *Hardy Boys* mysteries, each book in this 23-volume series is a positive-themed tale of human relationships, good sportsmanship, and positive influences—things especially crucial to young boys in the '90s. Through these larger-than-life fictional characters, countless young people have been exposed to stories that helped shape their lives.

WELCOME BACK, CHIP HILTON!

DUGOUT JINX
#8
0-8054-1990-X

available at fine bookstores everywhere